1st MAY 2009

Huckleberry Hawn

by
Cecil Horn

AuthorHouse™ UK Ltd.
500 Avebury Boulevard
Central Milton Keynes, MK9 2BE
www.authorhouse.co.uk
Phone: 08001974150

© 2008 Cecil Horn. All rights reserved.

No part of this book may be reproduced, stored in a retrieval system, or transmitted by any means without the written permission of the author.

First published by AuthorHouse 11/19/2008

ISBN: 978-1-4343-4900-2 (sc)

Printed in the United States of America
Bloomington, Indiana

This book is printed on acid-free paper.

My story covers the lives of myself and my two friends until we reached the age of 21.

Childhood. War years. Conscription.

Read on now.

Be a youngster during that tragedy and excitement, feel the intense pride in "just surviving" During those years, laugh a lot, maybe shed a tear or two, but I hope you enjoy the book as much as I enjoyed writing it, while looking back over those tremendous years.

*I*t was March 13th 1927, the sun was getting quite warm, shining from a clear blue sky, buds were breaking, birds were singing things were looking pretty good, but not quite so good inside No 15. Mum was in the bedroom, and in bed she was making strange noises, and shouting things like, this is the last time, no more, and when my father came into the room he was met by an icy stare and soon left.

That evening she had her baby, it might have been a time of great joy, but this was No 5 and to top it all was the same sex as the other 4, born on the 13th too, disaster!

I suppose Dad wanted a girl, so I guess I was not the flavour of the month, nappy changes certainly were not.

A national newspaper was running a serial based on Huckleberry Fin, the book was all about an American rascal of that name, and Mum quite liked the name, father whose popularity was at a rather low point, did not put up much of a defence, and so I was landed with the name HUCKLEBERRY HAWN.

Well it was great fun for numbers 1 2 and 3, number 4 was a little young too appreciate what No 5 was going to have to put up with for the fore seeable future, I think father did not know whether to sympathise or burst out laughing.

Well, things were pretty tight with four boys to feed, now there were five. I won't bore you by telling you with only two pounds fifty pence for his wages Dad found it tough, and I'll move on to that awful day when I was marched off to St. Mary's Primary School. I say awful because poor Mum did not know where to put herself. I was screaming and shouting "I'm not going, I don't want to go" fortunately in those days Mum was allowed to give a smack or two or three or four, my behind looked as though it had been left out in the burning sun for a while.

Mum was a warm hearted women, a bit on the large side, with a hand to match, but she did not often use it on her boys, she just pointed out to Dad which one required treatment. This was administered by a 3 inch leather strap, usually this had the desired effect.

Anyway I was bundled off to school and placed before the teacher, she was a very nice lady, and I took too her right away, especially when she said what lovely blue eyes I had. Unfortunately this was overheard by another little boy by the name of Raymond who gave out a nice loud raspberry, and then had to stand in the corner for his rudeness. Now I've had it I thought, he looks a right tearaway but when he came and sat next to me and said "ere, is that right, your name is Huckleberry and I said yes, he burst out laughing and was sent back to the corner. Well that's it mate I thought, 1st day, and I've made my first enemy, but from that day on he was my best mate, We had lots of fights but these were usually forgotten while planning our next escapade.

Mum continued to escort me to school, I think this was not so much for my protection as to see I did actually get there. anyway it was obvious resistance was useless, I would get walloped by Mum or thrashed by Dad if I did not attend.

My teacher in primary was very nice, she was everybody's mum, but the days seemed long until the sun shone through the round window, and its rays fell on the classroom clock, and it was time to go home.

After a few months Mum turned the escort job over to brother Herby, and after a year or two I managed to convince Mum I was old enough to get to school on my own.

Now to get to school I had to go by the 'black huts', these were as they were called painted black, built of rocks beautifully kept inside, but home to a number of boys who were always looking for a scrap. The fights usually came after school it would not do to arrive at school looking as if we had been up to no good. The head teacher seemed to understand boys very well, it was as if he could read our minds. and in those days the cane was perfectly legal, and always on show.

Getting through the black hut gang was most time no trouble but sometimes we met stiff resistance which usually meant hurling every available stone at the enemy, but there were seldom any casualtis though one of the enemy did suffer a direct hit fron one of our high altitude shots.

Mothers family is now complete she now as eight children, after myself (No5) she had two more boys before she hears those fantastic words, No, not I love you, though I'm sure she never doubted that, no the three words she had longed to hear came loud and clear fron the midwife as she delivered number eight, IT'S A GIRL!

Tears of joy filled Mum's eyes seven times she had been at this point, only to hear same call, it's a boy!

The call echoed around the house, Dad, it's a girl. Dad was in the front room, deep in thought and probably prayer. If it's the same again, his life will not be worth living.

He heard it, it's a girl [, He was sure that's what they said he leaped into the air and headed for Mum, and the beaming smile on her face said it all. Both with a wide grin and tears in their eyes, the relief of all those years was plain to see. Just which one thought was it really worth eight children to produce both sexes, I shall never know. Mum was so proud that she had done it, that she forgot the daily toil that would be her lot for the next twenty years. Father of course would spend the next twenty years making a fuss of his daughter in between dishing out the punishments to his seven sons.

Such punishment I only just managed to avoid yesterday. Herby and I had been kicking a treacle tin around the yard, great fun until Herby gave the tin a rather stronger kick, it rose into the air and caught me on the back of my head. This had an immediate reaction, I picked up the tin and threw, it at him. Unfortunately for me he was standing in front of the window, and my treacle tin went through the window, making quite a lot of noise.

Dad was in his 'dark room' which he used for his photography and so heard the breaking of the glass quite easily. Hardly had the tin gone through the window when I heard the dark room door opening and his shout of "heltobogon on thou clommo" which to this day I have never known the meaning. What I did know was that I had about 5 seconds to decide if I would stand and face father or get the hell out of here, I quickly chose the latter. My escape route was not clear at that precise moment but I hoped it would come to me on the way. So firstly I ran through the back door, through the living room, up the stairs into the back bedroom, now it might have been quick thinking or just luck but I I had picked the one bedroom from which I could escape.

The room had a lean-to shed built on the lower area, and I was able to open the window, and slide down the shed roof, and go like the wind down the garden, into the allotments at the back. Well I knew for the time being I as out of harms way and as it was early afternoon on a Saturday, and a summers day, I reckoned I might just think of an answer before dark, if nothing else I was an optimist.

It seemed a good time to see if Ray was coming out, and so I called round his house, he was not doing anything much, and so we decided we would go for a ramble over the warren.

Now I have not yet mentioned Steve, he was a great character full of wise cracks and laughs, a perfect member of the three musketeers we called round for Steve and off we went. We had not gone far when I told them what had happened, a slight mistake as it took some time before they stopped laughing, and as I still had not decided on my defence on reaching home, it was not too amusing to me. However it was a warm May day, and great fun. Every bush had to be searched for birds nests, trees climbed, jokes told and if they became a little personal the teller had to be wrestled to the ground and made to beg for mercy, after which we would go on our way.

On this day, our real destination was the rough ground where the Snipe builds it's nest, and we usually found them in the rushes quite easily. We had walked to this area bout two miles from home, the time had flown by, teatime had come and gone and it was beginning to get a little less light. We thought we ought to be heading for home and so we did, but two miles seemed a lot longer that evening, one because we were tired and two because I could not think what to say when I opened the back door.

We arrived at the top of the black huts and Ray and Steve went on to their homes, there at the bottom I could see our house. It was almost dark, it occured to me I could be in trouble for the time as well, I summoned up all available strength and in I went. Father stood up and glared at me, he would not take his belt off unless Mum said so, she was really the boss. They both went for me with all the words at their disposal, then the Mother appeared in Mum, and she asked what I had been doing, this gave me the chance to appeal to her motherly nature. With suitable rubs of the eyes and looks that appealed for clemency I saw the first signs that I might just get off with a strong warning. Father said what he would like to do with me, but Mum just said get up those stairs and think yourself very lucky, and I sure did! Needless to say my pocket money (1 penny) per week was stopped indefinitely.

Today was Sunday and as I could hear movement down stairs, and breakfast as being prepared I decided to join them. My entry into the living room did not seem to attract much attention, that was great. Dad was reading the paper, Mum was getting the breakfast and the two younger ones were scrapping over comics, the four older brothers would not rise until nearly lunch time.

Breakfast was somewhat quiet I had the feeling my popularity was still rather low, having finished my breakfast I was tempted to pick up the paper, but as it was just beside Dad I thought I would not push my luck, and so I went into the garden.

Later on it occured to me that Sunday morning was when Dad cleaned his rabbits out so it might be a good idea if I did mine. Mine were just two "Flemish giants' but his were prize winning "Chinchillas' and as he had won several prizes with them he was quite proud of them. Sure enough I could see Dad heading for his shed where he kept his rabbits, and as he came by I said that one of mine was not looking too good. He went over to my hutch, had a quick look and suggested I come into the shed and get some of his special food. This gave me the chance to say what lovely rabbits they were. He then went on to tell me where he would be showing his chinchillas this summer, and the prizes he was sure to win. Of course I agreed, and said how he could not loose. This seemed a good time to take the rabbit food and hope yesterday was well and truly forgotten.

We used to have to go to Sunday school, but after Sunday school last year we decided to collect a few walnuts from the vicarage, and some of the best nuts had fallen over the fence in a cemetery. Too tempting to leave them there we climbed over the railings and collected them, seen by our Sunday school teacher it soon reached Mother and after suitable treatment Sunday school was no more.

Early on Saturday morning the following weekend I got up and went on my own to the Vicarage for a few more walnuts, there were five large trees so the vicar would't miss a few.

There were quite a lot down and I soon had about four pounds of nuts. I decided that was enough and went on the road for home, I had only a few yards when out from the hedge stepped a copper. "What have you got there boy? well I did not have to answer he just took the bag, he knew what was in there because he had been watching me pick them up. He waited till I came out and the crafty swine took them for himself. Now when I read about bent coppers I remember that one.

That was last year but now It's Monday morning, Mum is calling up the stairs "get up or you will be late for school," I soon dressed and went downstairs, the room was still a big dark as the piece of ply wood was still where the glass used to be before my treacle tin, it was a slow walk to school, that treacle tin was still on my mind, and it was Monday. The day went by very slowly, even Ray's jokes didn't seem as funny as they did most times, but the day finally ended and home we went.

Ray was very keen to know what happened when I got home, and seemed very disappointed when I told him I got off with a caution!

Today when I arrived home I opened the gate and turned toward the back door, Dad was between me and the back door, but he had a grin on his face and a tin of putty in his hand. He had just finished putting the new glass in the window, that grin told me we were on good terms again, and I think he was as pleased as me.

He really only wanted peace and quiet, mostly he was in his dark room on his photography, no body was allowed in there because opening the door and letting in daylight in could ruin his photos. It was only on Mothers request that he was forced to administer the punishments, but when he did he was quite good at it.

It looked like being a dull week, but on Wednesday Dad had a call fron a national newspaper, there had been a murder about ten miles away and they would like a photo or two. He was on a retainer from the paper, it was his job to get to the scene of the crime, and see what he could get.

Fancy coming Huck? he said, and I quickly hopped into the sidecar. We had no luck at the victim's address but, the neighbour had been on good terms and was happy to part with a snap for a consideration! Dad would be paid if the paper printed the picture, and if they thought it good, and it covered two or three columns he was in the money. It was soon on it's way to London. Next day found him scanning the paper, and there it was with a story and the photo covered two columns, not only was he in the money, but I think he felt like a real reporter, he was rather a quiet man and something like this was exciting to him.

Friday has come round again and pay day for those allowed pocket money, that was the five youngest, the three oldest were workingand so did not get any. I of course had been banned due to the treacle tin, and so it was a little painful seeing the pennies handed round. When the last four had received their pocket money with a few grins in my direction, I was near to tears, when a penny landed in my lap. I looked up and Mum with a grin on her face said "don't tell your Father" and then it was grins all round. I was very grateful for my penny, but it still left me two pennies short for our Saturday morning seat in the Odeon, that was three pence, and so we would have to earn some from some where else. We decided we would go to Springets Lake and get some marsh marigolds that would be in bloom about now. This was quite a sizeable lake, and deep, but what we wanted were all round the edge! Having picked a nice lot we headed for our favourite customer, she was a lovely old lady who on opening the door would always have a smile. We called on her most years and so seeing the flowers she knew why we had called. I often wondered if she liked march marigolds, but I am sure she bought them from us not because she liked them, but because she was probably a mother and she liked the grins on these three urchins.

Our other means of income were 'penny for the guy' 'carol singing' and bobbins for fire lighting, Well it was not the right time for the first two, so it was bobbins next.

These were bundles of wood about eight inches long, these would sell at seven bundles for sixpence, we always managed to sell our entire output, but this was mainly due to the fact that our soap box on pram wheels carried a rather small load. Our overheads were not great as we would get our wood from the market, and should some of the contents still be in the boxes we were doubly pleased. The stall holders seemed to be more interested in us than the customers, strange!

We are on holiday now and finding it a little more difficult to decide what to do, but today we are going to visit Fred and Jim who live about a mile away. As we were in their territory we let them lead the way. Fred felt ten feet tall, a born leader of men. We would go down this lane, over the fence and keep close to the hedge so as not to let the man spot us, "ok lads?" Well it was a great day. The route took us along by the river, the day was warm and the river was not deep and so a walk in the river shoes and all was a must. We had gone quite a way and our stomachs told us it was near lunchtime, Boys in those days did not have watches. Freds route home was to take us across a field with a number of small wooden buildings which turned out to be hen houses. I think Fred had been here before as he seemed to know all about hen houses. As we approached one of these building he said that if we lifted the board at the side there might be some eggs. The thought of all our mothers being presented with some eggs seemed a nice idea, Fred said the farmer would not miss a few. He lifted the board over the nest boxes and sure enough in about eight nest boxes therewere about a couple of dozen eggs, we each had about four eggs, and continued on our way. We had only gone a short distance when a shout in the distance said "come back with those eggs". Now it was not far from the fence along the field and the man was more than twice the distance away, but he had one advantage over us, an alsation dog! The fence seemed the best bet, we ran like the wind, a quick look over our shoulders told us the alsation was catching us up, but we were nearly at the fence. The fence would be difficult, it was iron railings with sharp points at the top. It was an awful thought what one of those spikes could do. We all got over safely, completely out of puff, but well ahead of the dog, who now just stood and barked. Next thing was to get away from here and round to Fred's place, we were doing a sort of very quick walk, we had not checked the eggs but we had some very nasty thoughts. We came to the end of the lane, and into Queens Road, when a man came down the road on his bicycle, he stopped just in front of us, and leaning his bike against the fence fixed us with a gleeful stare, "You have stolen some of my eggs" he said "haven't you", sheepishly, we nodded in those days you did not run when caught, you stood and took your medicine. He asked why had we done it, well we said truthfully, that we thought our mums would be pleased. He could see by our appearance that times were not that good at home, but he was obviously going to make us understand what we had done. Do you think your mothers would be happy to know that they have thieves for sons? they think they have five fine boys, how would they feel to see you now? We felt lower than a snake, he could see what he had done to us, he had not laid a hand on us but he had done what he had set out to do. He was a nice guy, he could have had us in the juvenile court and perhaps started us on our way to borstal, a young offenders institution with a fearful record. "I hope you will take notice of what I have said and steal nothing again, now if those eggs are still not smashed, you may take them home to Mum, that's if I have your promise that you will not steal my eggs again"

    He had by now made us feel extremely small, and we all very quickly said we were very sorry and would never do it again. If that chicken farmer had thrashed us unmercifully we would have shown utter defiance, shouted at him all the abusive language we knew but what he did with his words stayed with me all week, and the following week we had an almost identical experience.

As usual we were discussing what we should do, this might take half an hour, but we usually agreed on one idea, this time it was to se if the chestnuts down "the drive" were ready. A little optimistic as it was only just September and chestnuts are not ready until October, but it was somewhere to go. So off we went up by the black huts, through the recreation ground, up by the school, down Magazine road, Gore hill and down "The drive". The drive led up tot he Grosvenor Sanatorium a hospital for tuberculosis sufferers, fortunately this disease has almost been irradicated.

Well the chestnuts were as green as grass nowhere near ripe and so the musketeer who suggested this particular trip was quickly subjected to a few choice words and on our merry way we did go. This took us across fields which today carry the M 20 motorway, how quiet it was before the M 20. We came from the fields across Canterbury road and turned down the lane running down to the river. On the way down the lane was a haystack, this was a stack of dry grass about 8 yards square and 12 feet high. this would e great fun. We soon climbed up ontop and then slid down, climb up, slide down again, we soon became bored with that and proceeded down the lane. There just off the road was a small brick building, and set in the walls were the bottoms of large bottles, green ,red and brown, they had been set in the wall as the little hut had been built. Unfortunately, to three boys like ourselves they were just targets, and soon there were three broken bottles. We had the shock of our lives when a rather large man came running out of the building, "come here you boys". As I have said before, when caught redhanded we just stood and faced it.

Why did you do that? you have ruined it! I can't reset them, the bricks were set around them.

This was the second time in a few days that a man had every right to thrash us, but I think the verbal thrashing had a greater effect. He must have spent half a hour explaining where we were wrong in destroying other peoples property.

He made it plain where we could end up if we continued that way, and then he said a few words that I have always remembered. Well you boys I hope that you will not forget what you have done today, but if you want to come down here and play, and cause no damage, then you are welcome to do d so.

Again we were left with a feeling like that of crawling under a stone, and we never did go back, he had shamed us in a few polite words.

The chicken farmer and the man with the bottles have by now long gone, but I am sure that the way these two men treated us and the words they spoke saved us from Borstal, the boys reform school. Had they thrashed us unmercifullyI am sure we would have gone back and in the process ended up in court.

Brother Bill is now eighteen and has just bought himself a motor cycle, it is an old "Excelsior" it seems to go well but it is no noisy, he works in a cycle factory about one and a half miles away and we swear we can hear him for half the distance. Brother Bill now has no need of his bycycle now and so he has sold it to Ern, No 2 son, who works at the local printing works.

Ernest's cycle is not as new but it is better than the one brother Les has. Brother Les works as a baker about a mile from home and so is happy to buy Ernest's cycle.

No 4 son is not working and so has no money, so the cycle sale comes to an end, but Les is a generous sort of lad and has given his old bike to Herbie.

Herbie's bike was made up of many old bits, mostly found on the local tip. in todays terms it would not pass it's M O T. Herbie's is a little better than it was on account of his involvement in a slight accident which might well have been fatal but for an incredible bit of luck.

Herbie had gone for a cycle ride, this took him along Godinton Road, at the end of which he came too a major road, Chart RoAD,

AND A HALT SIGN, AND A LINE ACCROS THE ROAD TO MAKE SURE YOU DID.

Herbie's bike had a little difficulty stopping and went over the line by about three feet. At this precise moment a standard eight motor car appeared and it struck Herby's bike. The front wheel went sailing up the road. I think perhaps Herby had not tightened the nuts holding the wheel, as although the wheel had gone, Herby was still sitting the bike. Front forks were on the road and Herby's feet were firmly on the ground. He was of course extremely shaken up, and when the driver of the car approached him he fairly shook. The driver asked him if he was alright Well, physically he was, but he could not immediately answer as Herby had a stammer. The driver gave him a verbal thrashing before he realized the problem.

Seeing the problem he stopped completely, and there was a long silence, before Herby said he was very sorry. By now the shock had set in and he was near to tears. The driver now appeared a little embarrassed and I think Herby's stutter had quite affected him. He again told him in a little more gentle way how near to being killed he had been. He then said "well it has not damaged my car and you are not hurt, and I am thankful for that". Then he held out his hand and said "now take this and have it repaired properly". Herby did his best to get out "thank you" before he went off.

So the cycle that Herby gave me was now in reasonable condition well the front end anyway. It would be very useful as I would shortly be changing schools and my new school would be almost two miles away.

I would not be needing it today as we had decided after much discussion that we would play some golf. Of course we had no golf clubs but the local trees had supplied some useful sticks which did bear some resemblance. The golf balls had been acquired on our trips over the Warren. This piece of common land ran along side the golf links and so we would walk through the long grass bordering the greens and we would usually find a ball or two,

On one occasion seeing a ball just by the rough, we picked it up and a very loud shout from a rather irate golfer made it plain that he had just hit the ball and was walking towards it. It was definitely not a lost ball, Anyway we set off on our way along Godinton Road down by Mathers Iron Foundry and across the railway crossing which led to Bailey's fields, Standing by the gates was a man in is mid thirties. He handed us some cigarettes. None of us smoked at this stage and we had difficulty understanding why he was going this. We went off across the fields whacking our golf balls from one end to the other. Obviously it was not a question of getting the ball into a hole, it was just to see who could whack it the furthest. We played this game for quite a while and the balls were lost more times than they were in play. The cows in the field did not help a lot, should one actually fall into one of today's fresh cow pats, one was tempted to leave it there. We did not know at this stage that the day was to have a very sad end.

After an hour and a half or so of fun and the usual slanging matches and a bit of wrestling we were getting near the railway gate. We noticed that the man was still there and looking very uneasy. He seemed to be looking all around him as if he wanted to be alone. It seemed as he looked at us that we were in the way. Suddenly he dashed through the gate, and kneeling down he placed his head on the railway line.

We thought he was listening for the vibrations of a train some distance away, However, the train was not some distance away and it thundered by taking the man withit. We had been so interested in what the man was doing that we did not notice the train approaching and we could so easily have walked into it ourselves as we started to make our way over the level crossing.

Naturally the man was dead. It was an awful sight. We were very young and we could not help wondering why he had done this. What could be so bad as to make him end his own life.

We quickly hurried away there was nothing we could do, and I don't think any of us could face looking at him again let alone pick him up. However, we did see a man on his allotment with his vegetables and I called out "Hey mister! There is a man dead down by the level crossing, He's just done his self in" He looked up and bellowed "Git orff ome you little brats".

It was only after the third attempt that he put down his spade and made his way down to the crossing, We did not go with him. I think we were all feeling very sick and were rather keen to get home.

When I told my family they laughed. "Some story" they said. They thought it was very funny, until I cried uncontrollably. I couldn't stop. They realised then that I was not story telling and they did their very best to console me, but I think they too did not fancy going to see what they could do at the crossing.

I suppose today we would have been given counselling, but in those days whatever trouble you were in ,you had to jolly well get out of it yourself, but I guess in those days life was tough and you really did stand on your own two feet, and if you fell cover you just got up again.

It's a warm day today and as it will soon be time to go back to school, we have decided to go to the river. We would most times go through Bailey's fields, but the thought of that man with his head on the line was still fresh in our minds. We chose instead to go down Gas Works Lane and through the railings into the fields where the Co-op kept their cart horses, and along the river bank.

Thr river was not deep but had two deeper parts, which we called the four feet and the six feet. Ray and Steve could swim but I could not, but we still had fun. Up stream was the 'ford'. This was a shallow crossing for carts to cross and be washed. Along the river were places for the cattle to come to drink and some would get right into the river and so it was not unusual to find while swimming, lumps of 'cow material' floating past. The swimming baths cost money and as we were always a bit short of this, the river was our best bet. Along the river we found a raft made up of oil drums and planks of wood. We untied the rope and 'set sail'. All was going well, we were singing that piece from Sanders of the river at the top of our voices, whilst using our hands as paddles. We had not noticed that we were slowly sinking. When we did notice it the singing stopped and all we could hear was the air escaping from the drums and making bubbles below the water.

On closer inspection we could see why we had sunk. The builders of the raft had carefully arranged the drums to that the filler caps were just above the water line. Then they had removed the caps!!!. The raft would e quite alright as long as no one stepped on it. As we had taken it without permission we did not know about the booby trap. This nearly cost me my life.

The Water Company had recently dredged the bottom at the point where we had bottomed out. and so the depth of the river had dramatically changed from 3 ft to 6 ft deep. After 2 or 3 yards, I dropped over the edge, and found myself in real trouble, because as I said earlier I couldn't swim! I shouted out to Ray and Steve who at first thought I was mucking about, but a closer look at me in trouble convinced them, and they quickly heaved me up the bank to safety. To me it was real terror, but to them it was a great laugh. This is how we were though ,lots of scraps and lots of laughs.

It's hop picking time and Mum would not miss it for thr world, she loved the laughs and the banter between the pickers who were mostly women. Saturday morning meant taking the chairs and baskets up to the "tank" where they would be collected by the owners of the 'Hop Gardens' and the people would sort them out Monday morning, when they would be given a number, and an alley. The hops were planted in long rows maybe two to three hundred yards long. They grew up strings to about ten to fifteen feet. The pickers would give a good tug and it would come down, and the hops were then picked, if they did not come down the "pole puller" would cut it down, he was usually a nice young chap, very popular with the ladies. The hops were picked in a 'tally' basket this measured about three feet across at the top, down to about two feet at the bottom and was about three feet six inches high. Now the hops were about an inch long and about three quarters of an inch round, and so the thoughts of filling a basket of that size with hops of that size did not inspire me at all. Mum would pick into the tally basket but myself and the three younger ones would pick into smaller containers and then tip them into the larger one. After picking a few baskets and doing a bit of whingeing Mum would be persuaded to part with a few pennies and I would make my way into the small shop at Kemps Corner. This would usually last until dinner time, in the meantime there was much to explore, and lots of new friends to make, and a few enemies.

At home if we were misbehaving Mum would inform Dad, but out in the hop garden she would defend us against all comers, she was quite a formidable woman. But there were very few squabbles in the hop fields and lots of laughs usually at a pickers expense, she in turn would get a laugh from another picker. The day would end with the 'tally men' collecting the hops and recording the amount picked for payment at the end of the two weeks which it usually took.

If we were lucky it might take a little longer and run over into the start of school. The last day was just to stack our chairs, baskets ect, and board the bus home which made a call at the 'Golden Ball' where the payment would be made for all the hops picked. Mums pay would be used for clothing to send the children back to school, four were now working ,but four were not.

A lot of what the pickers had earned would never leave the Golden Ball' and I'm sure the brewers were quite happy about that. I guess the pickers had too see what their hops had produced, and I think the beer some had drunk brought on the usual song, it went like this, depending on how much the singer had had.

Hopping is all over, money is all spent

How I wish I had never been
Hopping down in Kent.

It had been great, and really, it was a working holiday for mums who never had a holiday, who spent their lives looking after their family, and if you happen to have eight, as Violet had, there was very little time left for anything else. Although none of her brood showed any sign of being brilliant scholars, I think she was glad to see their happy go lucky attitude to life, in this way all seemed to take after herself.

Brother Bill is still making bikes at 'Normans; Ern is printing at 'Headleys' and Les is baking, and decorating cakes, but that is during the day. Quite often when Mum came down in the morning, there in the kitchen would be chicken, fruit, eggs, pheasants, all kinds of things seemed to materialise. Mum knew all about manna from heaven, she was in her younger days, a Sunday school teacher, but she was quite aware of just how these gifts had been made, she knew, which one of the three older ones was responsible for these "gifts". I think this particular brother was her favourite he had an impish grin, and a bit of a temper, but he would do anything for Mum, so she could never bring herself to give him the 'talking too' that she knew he should have. She obviously never told Dad, because she knew Dad would have too administer the punishment, well that for one thing, but there was another thing, Dad thought it quite miraculous what she did with the house keeping. To be occasionally served chicken, and pheasant, really impressed him, he never enquired 'how', he just hoped she kept doing it.

Mum had a really hard life looking after a family of ten. I guess she was really tough as old boots, and could see off anyone who said a word against her family, but one of the things I remember is, how she never sat down with us at meals, as she was always going from dining room to kitchen, and when she asked if anyone wanted more there was just one reply from us all, yes!

Dad was usually quite satisfied with his meal, his work was not hard, and so he had not a great appetite, the one thing he insisted on was the strongest cup of tea, nearly black. Mum used to say his inside must be as black as his hat. He was an excellent photographer, but he would never be rich, as he was a perfectionist and having taken a very good photo, would then spend more time removing the pimples and spots from the negative, making the subject more beautiful, but less profitable. This became even more noticeable when the subject happened to be a young lady in her late teens who would like a full length photo on the settee in her bathing costume, this picture would take a great deal of time and even more retouching, Having put his all into getting absolute perfection, leaving no cushion unturned he would be a little disheartened, when Mum questioned the time necessary to take a few photos, he could hardly say it was the number of positions she required! He knew she just would not understand, after all it was for a beauty compepetition.

Tomorrow we three musketeers will be changing schools so we shall be leaving St Mary's and the very nice Miss Arlin, she was just like every bodies Mum, I think we all loved her. Then there was the rather daunting Miss Luinn, and the rather refined Miss Swaffy. and a few more who really made a school where a child would happily go, and want to learn.

We shall be going to Ashford South Central, a much larger school, with a headmaster who was known for a good, but disciplined system. We shall feel almost grown up, ten feet tall, but this feeling will make us feel as if we are leaving another world behind.

Living on the North side of town we had roamed most of the area West to East. We would search for pheasants and Moorhens eggs in Godinton Park, chestnuts on the common, golf balls in the links, sledging in the warren and digging out bullets on the 1418 war practice area. On to Pledges fields for plovers eggs down to the river, and on to Wye, not all in one day obviously.

Wye was about as far as we went and it was there we did our only bit of climbing. A vertical chalk face, it has crumbled a lot since then, but at about thirty five feet high it presented quite a challenge, and I think we all felt a little afraid. I think the piece of grass I shall always remember was the handful I grabbed at the top of that climb, but of course none of us would let on that we were scared. So at eleven years old ,we are on our way to our new school.

Down Gas Works lane through the park into Jemmet Road, and there a few hundred yards up the road is this very large building. It looked so cold and unfeeling like a massive square box with hugh windows, the little school of St Mary's suddenly seemed like heaven. We went through the gate doing our best to look like three 'Al Capones' determined to show any tough guys that we were not to be messed with and eventually the whistle blew and there was no going back.

The new intake were taken to the gym and told to sit quietly, this of course almost impossible at eleven years old and the master in charge bellowed "BE QUIET"! The door opened and in walked a rather short man in his fifties, with a slight cough, "stand up" said the master ,hearing this, the other man said "right sit down" which seemed a rather pointless exercise. I am the headmaster here, my name is Mr Pumphrene if you come here to learn then you will leave here with a good education, the teachers here are as good as you or your parents could find anywhere in this town, but if you are determined to cause trouble to these teachers and undermine the efforts of the rest of the boys here then you will be seeing a great deal of me.

If you come to me in connection with your education I will do my best to help, if you are sent to me for punishment I shall be happy to oblige, and this is the instrument I shall use.

The other master handed the head this cane with a handle on it, there was an unmistakable grin on the masters face. "I hope I never have to use this" the head said, "but let me assure you all I can, now off you go, work well, and learn all you can, it is a had world out there, dismiss."

The master who had taken us in to meet Mr Pumphrene was Mr Nixon, and it was he who took us to his class. Wishing to put the fear of the Lord into us, he proceeded to point out to us, that while the 'head' had a very good way with the cane, he being quite a bit taller could bring this cane down with such a swish it would seem like a rifle bullet and on making contact with the target the boy would wish it was!

Bill Pumphrene I thought was not a bad sort of guy, he would use the cane to maintain discipline, necessary in a large school of boys so I gave him a tick, but Nixon I thought seemed to show a fiendish delight in the cane so I put down for no tick. Having had Nixons history class we moved on to Wiggy Tracey opposite to Nixon. He was an easy going chap, and if you did a reasonable amount of work, you were OK. I think the fact that he was in his fifties and did not show a grey hair in amongst his black mop gave the boys the idea that it was a wig, hence the name 'Wiggy' he also gets a tick.

Next we came to Bogey Battle ,he was our maths master, and like 'Wiggy' was a nice guy. He did however have one failing, he was quite fanatical about European language 'Esperanto'. This was a mixture of most of the languages of Europe designed to get anybody who used it across the continent with little difficulty About half the class would stay behind after school, and he would teach us to use it. I found it quite interesting, but now of course almost all the world speaks English.

The problem for Mr Battle was, that the boys quickly realised that a question about Esperanto in the middle of a Maths lesson meant no more maths,, and the time would quickly come when Mr Battle would say "good gracious is that the time? and off we would go to the next class, he also gets a tick.

This was Moggy Horgane, he was not very tall and a little rounded. Certainly he was decidedly lacking in humour, but he knew his subject and as it was my favourite subject, we did not really cross swords.

Mr Tereslord was our physical training teacher, he also had a nick name but as this might be read by juniors I shall leave it out! He was determined to throw us over 'the box' over 'the horse' climb the ropes, and generally see that we received as much physical exercises as he thought necessary. It was rumoured that he was interested in politics, (left of centre) and I think that while he was sitting on his behind reading his papers at weekends, we were getting ample exercise on our rambles over the fields, no tick for him!

We had two woodwork masters, Mr Quitten and Mr Richer, Mr Quitten was a nice guy quite the gent, round about 35 years old, Mr Richer was about 55 years old and quite the opposite, his main hate was any boy using a chisel the wrong way, this always resulted in a clout round the ears, quite painful! Alas I found it very difficult to mourn for him when during the coming war he was killed, no tick.

Mr Saniels was our metalwork master, he was quite a nice guy but he bore the appearance of a man who had seen much metal ruined in the interest of learning. He was a good teacher, he never went berserk like some. Good guy, a tick.

Lastly there was Mr Sarcro ,he was the art master, by his accent he was not from these parts, and I wished many times he would go back there, wherever it was. His greatest delight was using his 3 strap' on the boys, if looks could kill he would have died many times. Definitely No Tick.

Well you have listened very well with expressions of great interest, you may now boys and girls, all have your refreshments.

Here endeth the first lessons.

Well it has been a long week, a new school and new teachers who have been sizing up the new pupils like WE have them, so tomorrow Saturday we are going fishing! Now fishing in my case needed a little care and preparation. As I had two older brothers in my room, and as I would be getting up about quarter to six, They would not take kindly to being woken up as well! Another complication was Tinker the collie cross dog in the shed, if he heard any noise the whole area would be awoke and my popularity would reach an all time low.

This was avoided by a long length of string, running from behind the gate, along the wall, through the window, and then tied to the end of of my big toe. Ray and Steve would creep down the alley and give a few tugs on the string, I would give a tug back, and quickly get dressed while the rest of the house carried on sleeping, Opening the back door I then had to go to the shed where 'Tinker' was kept to get my bike, and with a few reassuring words to the dogI was off.

It was a lovely morning still not very light, the only person to be seen was the milkman with his horse and cart. He would dip his metal jug into his milk churn and pour the milk into the container left by the lady of the house, I wonder what the minister of health would say today?.

To get to our pond, we would be going along the Chart road to Bethersden, about five miles. The lead bike would keep changing and a few rude songs would pierce the morning air, so we were soon there. The pond was about a quarter of a mile from the road between two lots of trees, this was good as we could not be seen from the road, rather necessary, as we were not supposed to fish in this pond. Most times there was a race to get our lines into the water but this morning I was carried away by what I could see and hear. It was still only six thirty and the sun was only just risen, the mist was still lying over the fields. Every, green, gold and red leaf on the trees seemed to sparkle with the suns rays, it was a wonderful sight too see. There were also sounds. so rarely heard today. The cock pheasant, his call seemed so loud in that early morning. The woodpeckers, and the skylark, seldom heard, the sky lark would be high in the air singing at the top of his voice, almost stationary, hovering. These beautiful sounds would e against a background of absolute silence, save for the rustling of leaves on the trees. Today wherever you go there is always one noise which is inescapaoable, the noise of aircraft overhead, but all those years ago, there were not the aircraft going off to all points on the earth, and the blue haze of air pollution did not exist.

"Got One", Ray's shout brought me back to earth, he had caught a nice Roach, the first of the day. We caught seventeen between us and were very pleased with ourselves, but of course, it was much easier in a pond, than a river, or canal.

The morning soon went, it had been great, school was a world away, and Monday may never come, but the owner of the pond did! We had to make a hasty retreat, snatching our liens out of the water we ran to the road, and on our bikes that we had left in the hedge. When we thought it safe we stopped and dismantled our tackle. It made a rather sudden end to a lovely morning, but we always enjoyed a good chase, especially if we were not caught!

Our own gold mine, or at least silver mine:

It all started some years ago when we moved into this house, it had belonged to a rather eccentric old man, I suppose he was a sort of recluse. The house was somewhat unclean, and all round were papers and magazines, and mother being a sort of housework hurricane, the first thing to go were those papers.

We were given the task of collecting and burning them, of course every boy loves a fire, and we had a great time. Next day there was just a pile of ashes, and dad was wondering what to do with them. There were some old rocks in the garden, and so to cover the ashes, and get rid of the rocks, we made a rockery.

That as I say was a few years ago, and now it was just a heap of weeds. Dad liked gardening now and again, not too often, and today he was going to remove the rockery, and level it. As I liked a bit of gardening I volunteered to help. Having removed the rocks he proceeded to level the ground. Almost at once we began to find coins, there were sixpences, shillings, florins and half crowns.

Huckleberry Hawn

I was glad I volunteered. Dad picked up a half crown and went up to show mum, a bit of a mistakes, as he was overheard by brothers four and six and before we could say cash they were digging like mad, Dad sensed that the money might end up in the wrong bank, and called a sort of diggers conference, he said that while he was quite happy for us to collect the sixpences, the shillings, the florins and half crowns were going into his bank. Well as one sixpence was a considerable improvement on our Friday night penny, we had no hesitation in nodding our heads, and picking up our spades. Having made what we considered our fortune we left dad to it, and went to see mum, as the coins were somewhat black and we needed to get some scouring powder to clean them. We could not get them very clean, but at least they were quite clearly sixpenny pieces, next stop was ma Hooks general stores, she looked rather surprised at the three rather excited customers, and of course kept her eyes firmly on us. I had two 2 ounce bars of chocolate, and still had a penny change, Herby had eight farthing gob stoppers and 4 pence change, and Reg had a quarter of liquorice alsorts and 3 pence change, and still we had quite a few sixpences in our pockets. Dad had finished digging the garden, and had done very well, so we were all quite pleased, but could not help wondering how many ten shilling, 1 pound and 5 pound notes we may have burnt! Perhaps also between the papers.

It is now mid October and chestnuts should now be ready, and a cycle ride to Hothfield Common will supply some good size nuts. but I feel chestnut time will never be quite the same after this year. It had been a windy night, and there were plenty on the ground, and is always great fun to climb the tree, and shake some more down, anyway we had a good day and soon filled our bags. The highlight of chestnuting for me was to put some in a saucepan, and add some salt, and boil them until soft. When they were ready soft it was then possible to squeeze out the sweet inside, which to me was great until last night.

I had eaten quite a few and it was time to go to bed, but I thought it safer to take the rest upstairs with me, as in the morning there would be none left. It was an old pan not wanted by mum, and so I left the nuts in it, and put them under the bed, where I could hear anybody helping themselves. I woke early, and it was Sunday morning and the rest of the family were enjoying a lay in, and so taking care not to wake the other occupant of the bed, I gently slid my hand down and under the bed to my chestnuts. I put my hand in the pan to get a nut, and was surprised to find the nuts that were DRY, were now very wet, and it quickly dawned on me WHY they were wet. The brother who shared the bed with me obviously got out of bed in the night, and mistook my pan for the other receptacle which was ALWAYS under the bed. I was so annoyed that I quickly woke him up with a few choice words and said what he had done, but to him it was very funny, this made things worse, and a fight soon got started this very soon brought mum in who was hoping not to wake dad. Mum asked what it was all about ,when I told her he had urinated on my chestnuts in the pan under the bed, she also laughed, and soon the whole house knew about it, and there was no sympathy, just the advice, leave them downstairs next time! That was the last time I had boiled chestnuts, I couldn't face them after that.

Well there is not much fun to be had in Novemberand December but in a fortnights time it will be christmas, and the season of good will, but I am wondering if there will be much fun in Willy Pumphrenes office on Monday morning.

When we finished school today we were larking about as usual, and Ray said "How about a ride on the crossbar of my bike" well I had done it dozens of times, and thought nothing of it, on he got, and off we went.
Now to get home we needed to go through Victoria Park, a no Cycling area, and so we should have got off and walked, but we decided to risk it, but as we neared the end of the park we came upon the Head Prefect walking home. To make matters worse

he had the class sneak with him, and so I have a good idea that 'Sneaky' will be only too pleased to give the Prefect all the details to identify Ray and me, on Monday morning out presence will be required in Willy's office. Well the morning had gone quite well and as it was almost eleven o'clock we decided we were ok, but at eleven o'clock the master was asked if the Headmaster could have Ray and myself.

It seemed a very long time sitting outside Willy's office but eventually a voice boomed out and we very soon went in. Before we received what seemed to us the inevitable cane we had to endure a verbal dressing down from Willy. He said, "you boys have been at this school for less than three months, but you have managed to get to my office. My office has a great many things for me to do, and your presence here aggravates my position considerably and so I hope when I administer your punishment that you will make sure you do not return".

Riding two on a bike I am sure you know is against the law and any boy at this school breaking this law will receive what I consider the necessary punishment, and today that is going to be six strokes of the cane, right you are first! I was quickly dealt with and then Ray.

After such a lecture it was almost a relief, but not quite, it was certainly rather painful. As we headed back to the classroom we discussed the fate of Sneaky, the Prefect was a little too big for us.

On opening the classroom door all eyes turned in our direction and of course we tried to look like two tough guys but our hands were still burning a bit. And so the slight grin on our face did not give a very accurate picture. Sit down you boys and get on with your work said the master, but picking up a pen was a bit tricky.

The following week went by quite quickly as it was the last school week before christmas and it was great to think that we had got through our first term reasonably well.

The week before christmas was a bit of a drag, the weather was cold and wet, and so there was not much too do. Mum like most

Mums had the christmas puddings, cakes and our favourite ginger wine to make, and all the other eats that come with christmas and so she was a little strained.

Like most mums she would also be determined that although money was scarce, her boys and her girl would have a toy of some sort, the three older ones would get the usual stocking fillers. but the five younger ones must have their presents.

This year it seems the boys all wanted trains etc, and Rita wanted a doll, and so mum would do her best to see that Father Christmas delivered these items.

Train sets came in all sizes and prices, and so they would have to come within her price range. There was not a lot of spare cash and so she decided that the two older ones would have a Marks and Spencer half a crown set (12½ pence) and the two younger ones would have a Woolworth's one shilling and six penny (7½ pence) made in Japan. This would be bound to cause a few whines, but while she would like to give us the world, she couldn't. Now the difference between these two sets was about five days! The Woolworth's set would be abandoned with a broken spring on the first day ,but the Marks set would go for anything up to a week. Rita's doll of course with no mechanical parts, and loving care, would out last all the train sets. Christmas Eve came and on going to bed we would all hang our socks on the bedpost and after some time fall asleep. In the morning our sock would have acquired an orange, some nuts, bars of chocolate, hankerchiefs and anything that might help to fill it up.

The world outside would be absolutely still, not a sound, very few people had cars, and those that did would not go out on Christmas day. It was a day spent indoors round the fire enjoying a day of peace and quiet, well it is if you had not got eight children.

In our house mum was downstairs, and this meant that she would hand out our presents when we came down, an in case we should miss out, once one moved, we all moved, and soon the whole house was awake, and she loved it, the excitement, the noise, but above al the look on the kids faces was worth it all.

Dad and the older boys saw it a little differently a cup of tea and a little longer in bed was all they required, this they usually had as mum needed to get things started, The "front room" normally out of bounds was a buzz with train sets, also the living room, both had a nice coal fire with a scuttle full of coal beside it. One side of the fire was reserved for Dad's mum gran, she would not say much, but voice her disapproval if we were a little too noisy.

Mum would, like most mums, spend the morning slaving over a hot stove, and most of the dinner time, dishing it up to a large family with large appetites, she seldom sat down and enjoyed it with us, she seemed not to sit down until the Kings speech at three. This was a must, father demanded absolute quiet, and we all listened, the King always came over as a nice guy, and so even for us it was no hardship. After "The King", the radio would probably be tuned to radio Luxembourg where one would find music and comedy. This was usually acceptable to all of us, although father was sometimes rebuked for laughing too much at Max Miller's jokes, mum thought them a bit 'smutty'

The evening is now quite advanced and dad is taking Tinker the dog out, and taking gran home at the same time. When he comes back we shall have supper, usually cold pork and pickles and so to bed, not very exciting but a day of contentment where we were all together, the world outside might not have existed!.

There were no lines of expensive cars outside, the houses were all the same along the road. We seldom saw into each others houses, nobody went for foreign holidays and bored us with several roles of snaps, and so there was less envy and jealousy, and much more contentment, and contentment is happiness, even when one is very short of money.

It's Boxing day today, another nice lay in, a left over meal day, which meant less work for mum, and in the afternoon a trip for the family to the 'point to point races, which mum loved. To me it was cold and somewhat boring, but I suppose to her it was an inexpensive afternoon, and relaxing, we would come home a little cold, and mum would serve up the inevitable hot buttered crumpets to go with the cold pork etc. The coal fire would be a blazing mass, and if we happened to have backed a winner, there was added pleasure.

Another evening of Radio Luxenbourg, music and laughter, usually four of us playing cards, with cries of "stick, twist" or or "buy one" with disapproving remarks from dad trying to hear the jokes, and the day draws to an end. Nothing very exciting, but a family get together enjoyed by all, and although she worked so hard, much enjoyed by mum.

It is mid January now, and although we did not get our 'white Christmas' it has certainly made up for it Thursday, so will it last till the weekend?. Well it has not melted, it is still very cold and today is Saturday so it is off to the Warren with our sledges It is a little over a mile to the Warren, but there are several nice runs, we made for the best one, and had about an hour before it became too crowded, and not much fun. Our next slope ran down the hill beside the railway line. This was not the best of runs but up to now had not been used. It was quite a good run with the light fern poking through it, or so it looked. After a few "eeny meeny moes" I drew the short straw, and down I went. About half way down I managed to hit a small tree stump, not showing above the snow. I bounced off of this and on to the railway fence post, the sledge stopped dead, but I kept going for another thirty feet, luckily all I went through was fern and snow for the last part of my trip, well I'll do anything for a laugh!

It's February now, the snow has gone, but it is cold and wet, not much to do, just school and homework, our thoughts are mainly of the Easter holidays, School today however did have a little excitement.

When Ray and I went into the toilets who should be in there but 'sneaky' the guy who was responsible for our caning, we pointed out to him politely, that his sneaking to the prefect had resulted in our being summoned to Bill's office, and when he said "so what" we became rather annoyed, and without thinking of possible consequences we decided to even the score. We told hi his hair was in a shocking state and we set about washing it. Plenty of lather lots of water and he was as good as new.

He showed no appreciation, but said he would tell his prefect friend again, and we said that would not be wise, or words to that effect.

The next day we were again called to Bill's office, the same wait outside, I guess this was part of the punishment, then the fearful voice of Bill Pumphrene "comin you boys" In we went, he was obviously not in a very good mood, he soon made it plain that if we kept coming back, he could keep dishing it out. Now he said, this boy says that you held his head under the tap in the toilet, is that right?. Feeling that he deserved it we denied the charges, Bill repeated the charge, and on receiving the same reply said "right! hold out your hands" and canned all three of us, sneaky got some too! Well your hands were a bit sore, but we felt better inside, we thought justice had been done.

Riding two on a bike in those days was certainly wrong, but we thought six strokes of the cane was a bit over the top, but I think now we should have no more trouble with sneaky.

March weather is usually cold wet and windy, and today is no exception, boredom has set in. Christmas seems a long time ago and the spirit of good will has somewhat diminished, or so it seemed yesterday. The day was also a little boring, and my brothers and myself were looking for things to do. I found part of the track of one of the long since broken train sets, and seeing a nice red fire, I put the rail into the fire to get it red hot, not for any reason just something to do, I was gone some few minutes out of the room. On returning I proceeded to remove the rail from the fire to see if it was indeed red hot, but as soon as I had taken hold of it I soon let go of it.

One of my dear brothers who obviously had long ago forgotten the spirit of goodwill, had pulled the rail out of the fire, and carefully put it back in the other way round, so that the hot end would be ready for me when I came back. I let out a loud shriek, and mum and dad were soon enquiring of the problem. On hearing the reason ,mum took care of the first aid, and dad took care of the punishment and the peace and boredom descended on the house once more.

Today is the thirteenth and my birthday, there will not be a party, balloons hanging outside, cakes with candles, all the things one would see today, maybe a bar of chocolate if I was on the right side of mum.

Life in those days was more a question of "staying afloat" no trivial extra, just what was necessary, but it was that continuing fight for life which was the challenge. No time to stand back and say "if only" just get on, and do all you could with what you had.

In Germany and Italy two are standing out, Hitler and Mussolini, and they are causing much concern in the rest of the world.

Already Hitler had been involved in Spain where his bombers have been used against the 'rebels'. The rebels had few arms and certainly no bombers. Mussolini chose as his conquest Abysynia, now Etheopia. He sent his army and airforce against a people with very little indeed, save for their courage, and the spirit of their leader Halle Salassi. How we hated to see such oppression, even as boys we wanted to join in, but we had no idea what war was like. We heard on the radio, and read in the papers, about the 'Hitler youth' and we felt as if we too ought to be preparing.

Hitler is continuing to take back land the Germans lost in the First World War. Our leader is busy going to Germany, and coming back with worthless pieces of paper declaring "peace in our time" but Chambelin is gaining valuable time, which we so need, because we are so ill prepared.

To our parents war was a terrifing thought but to boys of twelve it was so exciting.

Not quite as exciting as fishing, and today we are off to the canal at Hamstreet. This is a nice stretch of water, but it is 'angling society waters' and one needs a rod licence, which of course we haven't got.

The usual careful preparation for early morning departure, plus collecting a piece of meat, which we had scrounged from the slaughter house, and which now had some lovely maggots with which to fish. The canal had many kinds of fish and we are expecting a great day, but before we start ,we have to prepare for a rapid departure should one be necessary.

We walk to s spot about a quarter of a mile from the keepers cottage, which is just beside a rough track, here we can see when the keeper is coming and make our escape. We had a great day, caught many fish and never saw the keeper, and Germany and Mussolini might have been on another planet.

Dad who had been in the RAF in World War One saw what he thought was too good to miss. An advertisement in the paper, said that by joining the 'Volunteer Reserve' a man would be paid several pounds a month, just to be ready should the need arise. Dad who was a super optimist, decided he would have some, and soon joined up. Now he would sit back and collect the cash. Had he taken more notice what was happening across the channel, he may not have been so hasty. He was after all a man in his fifties, but being a photographer he would of course be of great use as RAF ground staff, so I think his age was overlooked by the RAF.

Hitler continued to make his speeches, demand this, demand that, smash his fist on the table, and the people lapped it up. along with his speeches were the flags all around, and with this combination it was a simple matter to attract the masses to follow him. There were very few who stood against him. but some did, and some paid with their lives.

It was a grand summer that year, and our rambles were great fun, and when the end of the summer term came we were full of great expectations. We did not know it then, but it was to be the last carefree holiday we would know for six long years. But for now it was great to go fishing, to lie back in the sun if the fish were not biting, to swim in the river, or take a piece of sacking and trawl for fish, there was so much fun still to be had. All this fun was made by ourselves, there was no spare money to buy our entertainment. The money we managed to earn would take us to the "Odeon," "Palace", or "Cinema," for three pence, and if we went to the 'Palace' there was the added excitement of a chase from Fred the doorman. We would always look through his dustbins for cigarette cards, and of course in the process make some mess, and a loud voice would signal it was time to make a hasty retreat Fred could not run much but he had a go, he was a great guy.

When we go back in the Autumn I hope Mr. Nixone will have forgotten the last two days of term. The next to last day of term resulted in me and the boy on the next desk, being the subject of Nixones displeasure. The boy's name or 'nickname' was Rubber, and he had objectionable habit of spitting through the gap in his teeth. That morning I was the target, and I very soon spat back, but whereas his was silent, mine made a slight noise. Nixone who could hear a fly pass wind, immediatly fixed his eyes on me, and as I had not quite assumed my position, began beckoning me out to the front of the class. This earned me six of the best, which I thought a bit unfair, as it was not me who started it. So on getting back to my seat I looked at Rubber and mouthed "you swine" which immeddiately brought a snigger from him just loud enough for big ears Nixone to hear. Nixone did not have a great sense of humour, and by now had even less. With is long boney finger he began beckoning to Rubber, whose humour also seemed to have gone, while still enticing Rubber to his desk, he reached up to the top of the cupboard with the other hand and took down his cane. It was one of the few occasions when I had been an onlooker and seen the cane strike the target. Nixone had a vicious strike, and I seemed to feel every one, with a sort of gleeful satisfaction, but when he returned to his seat, I Didn't look up in case I laughed, Hawk Eye Nixone had us both under observation.

The next day the last day of term, was also a lesson with Nixone, who was our English teacher, and today we were being asked to give a five minute talk out in front of the class. Nixone would just point to any boy ,and the boy would begin his, talk out front. Well the finger now pointed at me, and with Nixones eyes firmly fixed on me, with his back to the class I began. Rubber had not forgotten the previous day. would do his best to pull hideous faces, to make me laugh, he always did. I knew I must not look at him, or I would laugh, but it was almost impossible, and eventually my eyes caught a look at him and it happened, I sniggered, I think Nixone with almost no sense of humor hated to see a boy laugh, and immediately asked me what I was laughing at, Rubber was just dying to see me get out of this one, and I explained that the story I was telling was just part of an amusing situation. This satisfied Nixone, but Rubber looked devastated, and when I sat down I could see a look of total disappointment and the smug look on my face, I knew would have Rubber tearing his hair out.

Before we started our next term however the whole world had changed.

Hitler had continued to march into the countries bordering Germany, giving all kinds of lies and excuses, and his next victim was obviously going to be Poland, and it was not difficult to see that this could not go on.
Mr Chamberlain our Prime Minister could now see that Hitler's pieces of paper were quite worthless, and so he gave Hitler an ultimatum, If you attack Poland it will be war between us.

Hitler had until 11am Sunday the third September to withdraw his army. At 11am Sunday the third of September the world sat around their radios, Mr Chamberlain was to speak. At that precise time he was announced, and began to speak.

I gave Adolf Hitler until this time, 11am go give me an undertaking that he would withdraw his troops from thePolish border, I have to tell you now that no such undertaking has been received, and therefore a state of war now exists between us. This was devastating to mum and dad, but to a twelve year old boy, and his friends it was a time of great excitement.

I jumped on my bike and went off to Ray's and as I stopped Roland's mother was just coming out of her house, I blurted out wars been declared!

Roland was another friend who lived a few doors from Ray, and his mother was a widow with three children, two boys and a girl, she never did seem very strong and at this time she looked awful and my excitement quickly died. It would not have occured to me that most older folk knew what war could be like, during the next six years I shall learn a great deal!.

The money for free that dad thought he was going to get, he was now going to earn. A letter from the air ministry has informed him that he must report to an RAF base in Bedfordshire. There are a no Ifs' or 'buts' if he does not go, the RAF police will come and get him.

Mother was in tears as he went, she was now the one who would have to feed, cloth, and discipline 8 children, 7 of them boys, 4 of those were bigger than she was, she must have seen it as an awful task.

It is now a week since war was declared and we are back at school, there is a lot of stupid talk about it all being over by Christmas, children have a lot of imagination.

Back in the spring our form master suggested a trip to a Zoo in Bedfordshire, and the date he proposed was in September as it would be a little less expensive, he could not have thought for a moment that by that date we would be at war with Germany. Now of course he must get the parents o-k again as there is a risk of air raids.

There has been almost no sign of war in this country so far although at sea ships are being sunk by U boats, and our soldiers are fighting the Germans in France.

Well today we are going and we are quite excited really looking forward to the trip, although at the time it was proposed I said that I did not want to go. Mr Battle our form master asked us all if we would like to go to a Zoo, all but five said yes. He asked why we five did not want to go, but none of us were keen to give a reason, well he said, you have until Monday to decide, and left it at that.

The day went by as usual, and it was time to go home, and the usual rush for the door was under way,, as I approached the door I heard Mr Battle's voice. "Hawn, could I see you a moment please" (there were no christian names in those days) I wondered what I had done this time, but it was not about my behaviour, but about the trip, "I cannot understand why you would rather be here, than at the Zoo" he began "I would be grateful if you could give me an explanation". I was not keen to do this, it was a personal thing, not the business of the school, however I proceeded to do so. I said "I have seen pictures of Zoos with animals behind bars, in cages staring out at people staring in, sentenced to 'life' with solitary confinement". They would never know the freedom that I had known already, in my twelve years as a boy, and hopefully would know as a man for many years after the war, I cannot bring myself to be part of that staring crowd.

"Well I respect your feelings Hawn, and I myself feel very much the same way, but the Zoo I have in mind is very different from the ones you describe. This is what our Zoo is like, and he handed me a booklet, sent to him by the people who ran the Zoo"

It could not have been more different from what I had said. the animals all had their own enclosures with grass, and hedges covering the tall wire fences, they were a picture of contentment. Seeing the absolute amazement on my face he said "well how about it! will you come? and will you try and change the minds of the other boys"? I had no hesitation, I said it looked great and I would like to go, and would see if I could get the other four to come. This I did ,except one, and when he said "no thanks" I did not try to persuade him, he like me was one of a large family, and with dad in the army, and army pay was about 175 pence a week!

Mr Battle thanked me, and said he was pleased, now all the boys would be going. All, I said, "Yes he said, the school funds would pay for Smith" but I always suspected that he himself had put Smith's money in, Bogey Battle was a good guy, and I now call him Mr Battle.

So off we go, the coach is a buzz with chatter,, there was a singsong going on, the two masters were chatting, probably about more serious things, that were going on in the world. We arrived, had our lunch and went around the Zoo, and the booklet was not wrong. The lions lay y awning in the grass, the tigers were sleeping on top of their huts, it was indeed a picture of animal contentment a wonderful day!

Time to go home seemed to come all too soon, but home we had to go. We were very soon asleep and it must have seemed very strange with a coach load of children, that not a voice could be heard. The next thing I remembered was voice saying we were home, and to get our things together. When he was sure we were in a fit state to leave the coach he said, "He hoped we had enjoyed the day and he was sorry to have to point one thing out, a three page essay was expected from us on the trip, goodnight boys"

When I arrived home mum looked so pleased you would have thought SHE had been on a trip I guess that's the way mums are. Having asked me all about the day, she knew I would be hungry, and I had a good tuckin to a mal I would have had if I had been there for lunch. While tucking into my meal dad was listening to the news, mostly about the war.

Soldiers were dying, and civilians were being taken off to concentration camps, imprisoned until the end of the war, and I thought of those animals, not like those I had seen today, but those in solitary confinement, those people, like the animals, had now lost that which I valued so much, freedom.

It's Monday morning and we are with Nixone for English not the best start for the week. He says he hopes we all have our essays with us and he calls on the comic of the class Tristrum to collect them. The pile of books is handed to Nixone and he very quickly counts them, only 30, who has not done his essay?
It may have been forgetfulness, or just Tristrum's way of getting Nixone going, but Tristrum suddenly remembers he had not put his own in with the rest, "Sorry Sir I have forgotten to put my own in Nixone was not amused, and accepted it with a look that could have killed, the slight smile on Tristrum's face did not help.

Tristrum was the class clown. Last term we were having nature study, and the subject was, animals and their mating habits. At the end of the lesson we were asked for our questions, Tristrum's was, how do worms do it sir? no answer just a scowl from the master.

When I arrived home from school today there was a marvellous surprise. There on the table was a parcel, and the writing on it said it was from Cadbury Bournville. I knew what would be in it, as we had had the same parcels before, there would be about ten different bars of chocolate from one quarter to one half pound each. Mum had left it on the table as I am sure she loved to see our reaction. Chocolate she certainly did NOT buy. This was a result of saving the littlt pink coupons in the tins of cocoa, this was a must for the family. Cocoa "cured everything," but we did not mind as every tin had a coupon, and one day a parcel would arrive, and today is the day. After tea, not before, it would be divided between the family, all had a piece of each bar, mum was a stickler for fairness, each share was guarded day and night till it was gone and with each mug of cocoa we would think of the next parcel.

It is Saturday and mum is busy trying to satisfy our usual hungry bodies, a seemingly endless task. As she does this dad goes by the window and comes in the back door, "hello Vi" he says and puts his holdall in the front room. It seemed a little abrupt, as if he was afraid mum would suspect something, but she just said "have you wangled another weekend pass"||This seemed to stop him in his tracks, "no, he said" this time I have a weeks leave".

Mum knew by now what sometimes followed a weeks leave, but she just said "well that is nice" The meal over ,everyone quickly disappeared, I myself went into the front room to ready my favourite subject, a gardening book.

It was not long before mum opened this conversation, why this weeks leave? You never mentioned it. This had dad in the position he was dreading. There was no way out, he had to tell her. "I'm afraid Vi this is a special leave, I have been posted to France. Mum burst into tears, "up to now you have come home on most weekends, now I am really on my own, with eight children to look after, I don't think I will manage, it's just too much" She went off upstairs, and dad followed, the conversation continued, he was doing his best to reassure her, but she was having none of it, she was I think really afraid of what might happen, especially to dad. The war would end, but if dad were killed, I'm sure she felt she could not go on. Of course she had to say it again, as she had several times, "why did you have to sign up for a reservist? You would still be here and I would sleep at night".

Every time mum mentioned that advert for the RAF reserve, it was like a massive punch in the stomach, he felt he had let her down. It was obvious he could not lift her spirits, and so he said he had a roll of film to develop, and went to his old time refuge the dark room. Here he would light up his fag, and do what he really did well, this he could control. The war, and his wife he could not.

It was a bad week, we were all a little on edge, conversation was short, mum was scared, and dad I think felt awful, not at going to France, but at leaving mum with so much responsibility. It was not the way he wanted to go, but Saturday arrived, and he must go back to his unit. He opened the door, "bye lads" he said, look after mum, and he hugged mum like he had the feeling ,he would not be coming back for a long time.

The following week we seemed to take a much greater interest in the war, there would be someone in France, whoselife, so important to our family, could be in danger. Boys seldom involve themselves in anything for long, and that weekend we decided to go for a ramble, we had not gone far when we met Jim. Jim was a nasty piece of work, but being a year older than us, we did not feel like telling him to get lost, and so he joined us. The route took us along the railway line and up behind Chapman's Ballast firm and as always on the look out for nests. I found a Goldfinch's nest. It was partially destroyed but one egg was still there. When I showed the lads, Jim said he wanted it, but of course, nasty bit of work or not, he was certainly not getting it!

Jim then suggested that we get up on Chapman's roof, to look for Sparrow's eggs. This was agreed and I put my egg in my shirt pocket and off we went. We were soon up on the roof, and the next thing was to lay flat on our stomachs, and feel under the roof. No sooner had I done this, I realised why Jim had suggested it, there was a nasty wet place where my Goldfinch egg had been. It might have been coincidence, but I think he planned it that way He knew lying on the roof would crush the egg in my shirt pocket Jim must go!

He seems to think that we ought to be taught some of his criminal ways, we were just too law abiding. But one of the things I hold most important is that no matter what bits of mischief we get up to, the parents of we three shall not be shamed. Twice he could have brought this upon us.

We were outside the sweet shop, when he came along, and as usual considered himself invited. In we went for our sweets, and when we came out, Jim showed us a tin of fifty cigarettes he had stolen, "it's easy" he said. The people who ran the shop ,were the son and daughter of a jolly nice man, who died about five years ago, and I felt rather ashamed. I had just one thing to thank him for, as he handed the cigarettes round, I was convinced I hated smoking and I never have smoked.

The next time Jim could well have had us all in the police court was on one of our rambles.

We had gone about two miles when we came by a tennis court, and by the side was an old railway carriage, used as a club house, obviously with a few goodies inside for between games. There was a large padlock on the door, and of course Jim said "I could soon break that open". Nobody made a comment, but he was going to show us anyway. He picked up a large piece of wood, and with a massive clout the lock broke and in he went. Inside there were cigarettes chocolate and soft drinks, Jim was busily filling his pockets. Seeing we were not doing the same, he picked up three bars of chocolate, and threw one at each of us, "ere, av one its good chocolate" and to my shame today, we all ate it. That convinced me that Jim must go! I said to Ray and Steve, the next time He comes around I shall not. We all agreed that should the occasion arise, we would be about to go out with our parents. He seems to have got the message, he has gone back with his fellow criminals. I feel a little more at ease, there is a big difference between a bit of mischief, and breaking and entering.

We now have evacuees from London. They are not too popular with the local boys, as they all look like "little Lord Fontlaroys in their lovely light blue uniforms. It is not long before the Ashford Urchins take on the London Lords, and with their silver spoon upbringing, they did not put up much of a show. We were not too impressed when it was decided that the Catford Cuties would have our school in the afternoons, leaving us with just the mornings, not only that but some of the time we had to have our lessons in the local 'Freinds Meeting House' in Hempsted Street. But boys will always look for some advantage, and of course, it meant that we could probably do our own thing in the afternoons. But it was decided, that in the afternoons, we would take a look at some of the local industries, such as the Leather Tannery in what is now known as Tannery Lane, Here life was really just one round of work, carried and the Electricity Generating Station in Victoria Road. These were quite interesting, but of course there were not that many of these factories available. When we had visited all the available sites, we were hawked around the countryside. It was on one such afternoon, that we had decided it would e very boring, and we thought, we would do our own nature ramble, and we went to our favourite area 'Bailey's Fields' down by the river. We were quite enjoying ourselves, when in the next field we saw a long line of boys with Mr Battle at the front. This was somewhat embarrassing as we ourselves should have been with them. However by getting low in this dry ditch, we were out of sight, and Mr Battle and his boys marched on by. It was a bit tricky for a moment, but a great laugh afterwards.

Looking back on the arrival of the Catfod boys it seemed a rather stupid idea, to send them to Ashford, 54 miles from London, 54 miles nearer the German airfields, I suppose governments never change.

Six months have gone by since my excitement of hearing war declared, and it has not proved at all exciting.

We have lost an aircraft carrier, destroyer, and many merchant ships. War has already lost its excitement, we all think of those who mourn for those sailors killed on these ships. Poland has been over run, Finland at the hands of the Russians, Norway by the Germans, and now the Germans are moving into Holland, Belgium and France.

Mum has had a letter from dad, and she seems quite happy, "Dad has had an accident" she calls out. She is of course not happy about the accident, but because he is being sent back to England for treatment. as he has hurt his back and leg.

When the Germans began to move into France, it was decided to move dads base back a bit further from the front. Everyone had to help move the equipment, dad had just climbed onto the truck, when the officer said, "OK Jones move it up a bit" and dad fell out of the back. That was a couple of weeks ago and he is now enjoying some sick leave and mum is much happier..His accident was both bad luck and good luck.

He was unfortunate to have hurt himself by falling out of the truck, but he was so very fortunate to have got back to the U K before the Dunkirk evacuation. I do not think he would have made it, as he was by no means a young man. What these men had to do do to be snatched form the Germans jaws was a somewhat frightening thought. Having fought their way back to the French coast, they had to wade out in the sea, up to their chests so that small boats could take them to the destroyers further out, all this under fire. The men would then be landed in England given a mug of tea, etc, and a few goodies like bars of chocolate and put on trains, for camps further inland.

It was while playing by the level crossing at our favourite play ground 'Baileys Fields' that one of these troop trains had to stop for a signal. What happened then, to me was very touching. These men who had been through hell, were having the usual banter, and we and they were having a laugh. As we did this, they threw down to us kids, the chocolate they had been given by the Salvation Army, and other groups when they landed a few hours ago. This still brings tears to my eyes, they were great soldiers, beaten only by superior equipment, not by a superior army.

Mum's mother died many years ago, but mum still goes to the cemetery to tend her grave, and that is where she had gone this evening. She usually goes on her own or takes one of the youngest with her. I think it was not just to end the grave, but just to sit and think.

Her life was really just one round of work, carried out in a very noisy atmosphere. Here there was absolute quiet, just the song of the birds, not even the drone of aircraft, that invades all our lives today. It was such a lovely summers evening that as she sat there soaking up the evening sun, absorbing as much of that wonderful silence, as she possibly could, she heard the cemetery gates being shut, the gate keeper saw her hurrying towards him and waited, "thank you", she said, and went on her way to her rather noisy home. But in her home ,were her seven boys, and Rita her girl ,and at the moment Ted her husband, so it was still good to get home.

Hitler's generals stand gazing at the land across the channel so near and yet so far. Goering thinks he has the aircraft to bomb us into capitulation, Doenitz thinks his U boats ,by sinking all our ships, can starve us, so that sheer hunger will make us give up. Hitler thinks his army will quickly bring us to surrender, but Winston Churchill says that no matter what they throw against us we will NEVER surrender!.

Churchill made some memorable speeches that stirred the whole nation, they made us feel that the Germans would never set a foot in our land. They were preparing a landing force and WE had to prepare, the beach where once we had made sand castles, was now covered with barbed wire and concrete tank traps, and soldiers made sure we did not get any where near it. By the look of the beach the ships being lost, and bombs now beginning to fall on England it is becoming clear, that the war is getting closer. So close that the government has offered all those who were not in essential work, evacuation. Obviously this only applied to women and children and as my two friends were going, I thought I would be rather dull here on my own, I could miss a lot of fun.

It was a little difficult at home, as I was the only one of the four younger children who wanted to go. Mum did not really want me to go, she had decided that the family could stick together, but in the end she said ok. My case was packed, and the door was open, but I felt awful, she had tears in her eyes, and it seemed I was deserting a sinking ship. At the station the platform was packed with parents, the children were all on the train, the whistle blew, and the train pulled away. Every window had two or three heads sticking out, with hands waving like mad, a hundred voices shouted "bye mum" and mum on the platform with her handkerchief. An awful time for all the mums, but as Ashford station disappeared from view, the whole train was a mass of childrens voices. Mostly boys excitement, but by the end of the day it would be different, they would be thinking of mum, they had no idea what they were in for!.

Their destination was Oxford, and after a few problems on the rail we did get there. We thought that the bed we had left at home would simply be replaced by one at Oxford, but this was very far from the case. We were taken to the town hall, a very large building in the centre of Oxford, we filed into the hugh doorway with our possessions, but there was not a bed in sight. We were told to find ourselves a position on the floor, or on the balcony above.

What a sight! The whole floor covered with childrens bodies, with a noise like feeding time at the zoo, mum seemed a thousand miles away. Of course we were very tired and soon most were asleep just a few, for whom it was too much, and they just had to have a few tears, not for long, then the enormous building was silent. What an awful sight all these children uprooted from their parents sleeping on a hard cold floor, the only good thing was their mums could not see them.

The next thing was to hawk them around the streets, knocking on doors, trying to get people to take them in, this unfortunate lot fell to our masters at school, and it was obvious there was no rush to take us in. I think if the master had been in the door to door selling game, he would have decided to hand his notice in on the next day.

We were getting to be a smaller group but it was a slow process. However my luck was in! around the corner came a youngish woman, late twenties was my guess, and she looked quite pleasent none of that big stick stuff, "Hey Ray she looks alright" Ray looked up and slowly agreed, he like the master had nearly had enough, I think we all had. The lady was obviously heading straight for us, one of us looked like having a bed for the night, that would have been an improvement. Last night will be remembered for the rest of our lives. She walked up to the master and said she would take one of the evacuees. Thank you madam said the master "have you one in mind?" "Yes she said" I think I will have that one there, and she pointed to me. This was great, I was very pleased for a moment, but then I realised that the reason for me coming, would no longer be there, Ray and me were a good team. I said "thank you very much ,but I rather wanted to stay with my mate Ray" she looked very disappointed ,she had come from a house which was two streets away, and when she had offered her home, it had been turned down. I also felt very uneasy, the masters job was bad enough without boys refusing offers. I turned on my best disarming smile, and opened my big blue eyes as far as possible, and she smiled back. "Oh alright then ,but I dont know what my husband is going to say" ,and to this day I never knew what his reaction was to her. She took us to her three up ,three down, terrace home. Her name was Joan, the house was No 15, and the street was Albert Street, inside this terrace home, it was beautifully kept, not elaborate in furniture or decoration, but spotless bright homely atmosphere. It has long since been demolished in the name of progress, but I can still see it just as it was. She had two children of her own, one of each sex and so it as not going to be easy. It was fortunate that the girl was only three, her name was Jean, and the boy David was just six,
I think she was a little uneasy ,she was a little worried about Bill's reaction. She had some difficulty in persuading him that they

ought to take in an evacuee, and she had gone and taken two! She was of course very persuasive while she was in full flow, she would have this devilish grin on her face, this usually demolished any opposition.

Bill her husband was a quiet chap, and did not argue with her a lot, I think he knew where he was well off. She settled us in the chairs and fed and watered us, she usually did this well and asked us what was going on down in Kent.

This took care of the time before Bill came home from the car plant (British Leyland). When she heard the door open she quickly rose and went to the passage, and gently ushered him into the kitchen, where he would wash before tea. This particular night it took a little longer, as the explaining and the protests at being sort of conned. made Bill a little unsure of the procedure.

Joan introduced us to Bill and he did his best to make us feel welcome, but I had the distinct impression that his dear wife had him up in a corner, and he was a little displeased. He was an easy going guy, and when he came home next evening he was fine, asking us loads of questions about what was happening down in Kent. Glancing out of the corner of my eye it was obvious that Joan was much relieved, she usually got her way, but this time I think she felt that she had pushed 'Bill a little too far. Of course there were schools wherever one went, and we were told to report to the school in St Aldates, Which was about half a mile away, what had happened at Ashford was now going to happen here. We had to share the school with Oxford children and of course there was not enough room in the school for us all.

In Ashford we spent the afternoons looking at factories, and going for rambles, and in Oxford we were taken around the universities, I can honestly say that I have been to 'Balliol University', Magdalene' 'Christchurch' and a few more, but sadly only to look over the buildings, it was however something I shall always value.

We have been here nearly a month, not much happens here, just the odd scrap with the Oxford lads, and when mum's letter comes telling me what is happening in Kent I get a little down in the mouth.

We did have an exciting day yesterday, but I fear it was a another black mark for the Ashford boys in the eyes of the Oxford people, though I hope few got to hear of it. Six of us decided to take a walk down along the Thames, it was quite a nice day, and we had walked about half a mile, when we came upon a boat tied up to the bank and and it was not long before we all went 'aboard, It was a flat bottomed boat ten feet long, and we had a whale of a time acting the sailor, but one of our crew had untied the rope, and we realised we were moving away from the bank. We very quickly decided to 'abandon ship' and we soon jumped to the bank, well that was all except one, and he was too late, as the gap was now too wide. There was a look of panic on his face as the boat drifted out into the river. It was made worse by the fact that a pleasure steamer was on the same course as he was, and it's hooter did not help a lot, it just put the wind up 'Dragee'a little more. Fortunately, or maybe not, depending where you were standing the boat drifted to the bank on the other side of the river, and the pleasure boat with a couple more 'hoots' went on its way. This left Dragee in a rather difficult position, he needed to get the boat and himself back to our side. He decided like the true sailor he was (he was in the local sea cadets) to find himself a paddle and work like hell to bring the ship back safely. He took a piece from the fence and 'set sail' it was quite incredible his piece of wood was not very wide, but with a great many strokes to the minute, he did it. However his courage and devotion to duty did not get the cheer he expected. His mates, myself included, had seen this rather irate gentleman cycling down the towpath at great speed, and he seemed to have his eyes fixed on 'Dragee' So it was thought by the rest of the crew, that there was no point in us all getting thumped, and so we decided to "heave too" further along the towpath. The gentleman very nicely took the rope from Dragee and secured the boat, and I think Dragee thought that was nice of the man. However the man let loose with all guns blazing and told Dragee that it was his -------------boat, and with a few cuffs around the head, and a rather heavy boot connecting with Dragee's rear end, the man requested that Dragee--------------------------off back to Ashford! Not at all polite I thought, Dragee had been on the end of some rather bad language, and was more than ready to impart some of this to us, it took some time to repair our friendship.

Joan and Bill could not have treated us better. They were great. Joan fed us on the best she could buy, plus what was in her store cupboard, some of which she would not be able to replace, as things were beginning to get a little difficult to obtain. Bill would take us on walks up in the surrounding hills, he would also take us fishing, he made us a snooker table, he did what many fathers would not make time to do. So whatever he said about Joan bringing home two evacuees instead of one he soon forgot, great guy.

When we went out in the evening, we had to be home by eight o'clock, last night Ray decided he was not coming home at 8 oclock and when he did come home Joan read him the 'riot act' and sent him straight to bed. She had a heart of gold, and I could see she hated herself for what she felt she had to do. Bill was also uneasy he was a guy who got on with everyone, and any upset quickly showed on his face. After a while Joan asked me if I would go round the fish shop, and on my return she asked me to call Ray down, and we all had our supper and the happy family atmosphere returned. It was because we were treated so well, that Ray and I felt awful when we talked of going home. We were a bit homesick for our family and especially 'the action'

Tomorrow we are being to the Oxford Theatre to see Wizard of Oz, quite expensive for six of us, and all these things made it harder for us, but Ray has decided that he will ask his parents to come and get him. When he told Joan she was very upset, she was not cross, but I think she was so hurt, she had done so much for us and now we wanted to go back to what in her eyes, a very dangerous area.

She asked us "why do you want to go back to that?" I guess she as a mother could not see ,dog fights in the sky, anti aircraft shells exploding in the air, bombs falling, (always on somebody else) never on ourselves, checking out suspected German spies, all these things were so exciting to us, but so awful to a mother.

It's been rather a strange week, a mixture of quiet and laughter, quiet when Joan was thinking about loosing part of her family, and laughter when she jokingly ridiculed our wanting to return to 'bomb alley' as it was being called. Bill would just carry on reading his 'Oxford Mail' I think he was really on our side but he was not going to risk the wrath of Joan, I was glad of that because they did get on so well.

Today I am going to school on my own as Ray went home at the weekend, and it is already feeling pretty grim. I don't think I can stay for long now, I have asked dad to come and get me but have not had a reply yet. Dad is still in the RAF and so it will have to fit in with his own programme. In some ways I feel I have let everyone down, mum and dad by wanting to come here, and Joan and Bill by accepting their marvelous hospitality, and then wanting to go home.

I think they understand what is in the mind of a thirteen year old boy. The German air activity has increased, so has the excitement. It is of course only exciting, because we have not yet come face to facewith the bloodshed which has been the lot of so many at the hands of the Germans.

A little light relief today as Melba has come to stay, she is a very lively young lady of seventeen and at the moment there is never a dull one. I think she might help the week on its way, and I reckon I am going to need that. Yes the week was quite a laugh, and I was almost tempted to say, she was great, but today I have heard from dad, and he will be coming to get me next weekend. Melba went home yesterday, but Joan's sister Iris is coming to stay on Monday. I am sure glad about that, it will make next week end a little easier. Iris like Joan had a good sense of humour and we did get on well, but she like Joan could not see why we would want to go back, and that was really not a bad thing as it made some lively conversation and stopped me feeling such a rotter.

Iris I suggest is still hoping that sister Joan will at least keep one of her evacuees, and so draws her husband into the conversation, but Jim is rather a sporty type, who has a large motorcycle combination, and is as tough as Iris. He like Bill, has a great feeling for his wife, but he is also a guy who says what he thinks and Jim says that Oxford is a great place, but he can understand how youngsters could perhaps find it a little short of excitement, and by the sound of things it is getting somewhat hotter down in Kent. Well that just about finished that topic of conversation, his popularity dropped considerably, and he quickly asked Bill about the car plant.

Bill sensed the urgency, and launched into a lengthy account of a rather boring day on the line, but it did the trick. I picked up the 'Oxford Mail', Jim and Bill talked factories, Joan and Iris had domestic situations, husband and children, and so to bed, which had not come too soon. I felt very uneasy, as it was only three days to the weekend, when dad would be here to get me. They were indeed three very long days, there was not even school to go to, as it was the summer holidays. I never thought I would ever rather be at school, but it would have made the days shorter.

I thought the world of Joan and Bill, and the children Jean and David, and I think they knew that, but understood why I wanted to go home to my family, and the small market town of Ashford. Nothing much happened in Ashford apart from the occasional bombs, machine gunning from low flying Gerry's, crashed aircraft etc. And of course the shout from the Air Aid Warden. If he saw the slightest crack in the blackout curtains, no light must be seen from outside in case 'Gerry's Bombers' saw it.

Today's the day, my case is packed and Joan is doing her best to raise a laugh, she was very good at that. The last thing she would want, would be for me to go off without a grin on my face. Dad has arrived and with him he has my young sister Rita, she is just seven and as pretty as a picture. Joan would have quickly swapped me for her. We all had a cup of tea and a cake and it was time to go. With one enormous hug and kiss, I left the home from home I had known for a very short while, Ray and myself had been very fortunate to have known Bill and Joan, and to have lived in that small terraced house 15 Albert Street.

It was about one hundred yards to the corner where we would be out of sight, I waved and she waved, for that short distance, and with one extra burst we turned for home. It would not be the end, for we would stay in touch for the next fifty years, until unfortunately, she became a little forgetful, as she was now a rather old lady.

We made our way to the railway station and waited for what seemed ages for the train, though of course it was not, I was just impatient to be home. It was good to hear the clackety clack of the train wheels as they passed over the joints in the rails, I don't think we would hear it now as I believe the rails are continuous. On the train I wanted to know all about dads work in the RAF but he would say very little, With a compartment full of people, I think he was slightly embarrassed, and of course wherever one looked there was a poster saying 'careless talk costs Lives', which was very true. The odd sentence picked up by a German spy, could be the death of our servicemen.

I soon left dad to his paper and tried to find out from Rita what was going on back home, but I think her dolls were a great deal more important than the war, and so I contented myself with the view from the window. It seemed a long time before the train slowed to a crawl, and eventually drew alongside the platform and a very leisurely sort of voice said Ashford, Ashford, typical of our quiet market town but it sounded great to me.

As we left the station we passed the 'Cinema' where I had spent Saturday mornings watching films like 'Roy Rogers and his horse Trigger'

We were sometimes a bit short of cash, and had to pool our resources to get enough for one ticket which was 3 pence. Which ever one of us went in he would then go to the toilets where the emergency door was and let the other two in, all for one and one for all a great team. The Cinema is now gone.

Next we passed 'Tutts Nursuries', this was like today's garden centres but the trees etc, were a little more mature. Running along by Elwick Road were two rows of fruit trees, and I particularly remember the pears. They were hugh, golden and juicy, but there was a slight problem, we were easily seen from the other end of the row. and a quick sprint was necessary now and again, (also now gone). Further up Elwick Road we passed the conker field, the conkers were whoppers ,and won many a contest, and brought about many a scrap if the loser felt unfairly beaten, (also gone). Next was the big green gates of the market, this was the most important market in the area, animals and produce would come from many miles around. Smart stall holders from London, chicken farmers would bring their poultry, these would be in small cages waiting for auction.

We would walk up and down the row, and now and again an egg would appear, the cage door would quickly be raised and the eggs would be delivered to mum. The market was also where we had our first experience of dairy farming. Seeing a number of cows in the pens awaiting shipment by train, we thought we would do a spot of milking, well we went through the motions, but not a drop of milk appeared, I now know a little more about cows!

Twice a year the market would be ablaze with lights, and the organ music would be heard all around. The Forest fair took over with dodgems, chair planes and so many things that made it a must for your youngsters. The atmosphere was marvellous even if we could not have many rides. In December there was the fat stock show with the large animals which would go for meat, there were also beautiful Jersy cows, and a now and again mum would send us down for a bucket of milk, it was like cream compared with today's milk. (The market has now also gone)

Across the road was the ('Corn Exchange) here the farmers would do their corn deals, but it had so many other uses it had a large floor space and so it was ideal for dancing. It housed the wrestling bouts, quite big names were billed, much fun was had at election meetings where one could 'Heckle' the politicians, roller skateing was also held, so many things to do, it was a great loss to the young people of the town when it too was demolished.
We turned the corner into Godinton Road we would soon be home. We pas the tobacconist's where Jim stole the tin of fifty cigarette's, next was Goodwins the bakers, here I would be sent by mum for a loaf of bread, but it had to be yesterdays, as it was a penny cheaper, 3½ pence, instead of 4½ for fresh bread.

Now we are passing the 'Goods yard' which was where the railway parcels etc were distributed from, it was also the entrance to the coal yard. How sad I felt, as I watched those lovely big cart horses slipping and sliding on a frosty icy morning, as they pulled those carts loaded with coal up the hill from the yard. Next to the coal yard was the Gas Works, where coal was heated to a certain temperature to make 'coal gas' this was then stored in those enormous Gasometers'. What was left after the gas was extracted was known as coke. This was another job for me, with our soap box on pram wheels I would go for a shilling bag of coke, our own bag of course.

We are now passing 'Stanhay Agricultural Implements' where I shall spend some of my working life repairing vehicles for the ministry of aircraft production, until it is destroyed by a bomb. All thses buildings and places are now gone in the name of progress, but as we turn the corner our house is still there. I leave dad and

Rita and rush down the alley and through the gate, almost licked to death by Tinker our collie cross dog, through the back door, and there was mum!.

There was not a lot of hugging and kissing in our family, but one of her arms went around me and almost crushed me. The look on her face said it all, we were all together again, and even dad was here, although he would be going back to his base tonight. Dad has finally caught up, and has come in, "thanks dad" I said "that's alright my son, glad to have you back", and it was great to be back.

Four of my brothers were there ,and did their best to stir me up about going on 'holiday' when things were hotting up, but they really just wanted to raise a laugh, and make me feel at home, it was good to be one of the family again.

Brothers Bill and Herby were at work, although it was Sunday, the war meant that their work was of the utmost importance, and so they were working daylight to dark.

The summer has been hot and sunny and the corn fields are seas of gold in more ways than one, every grain is needed, if as an island we are to survive, Hitler believes he can, with his U boats at sea starve us into surrender, so Herby and Bill are cutting the corn that will make our bread. This they will do with a machine that bears no resemblance to our modern combine harvester, It will be cut and bound, and then stacked into large corn stacks, and then later it will be thrashed by another monster to remove the grain, the latter being a very dirty dusty job. During this period mum's bedrooms would be very messy, with straw and chaff, and of course the boys were not at all domesticated.

Harvesting during this Battle of Britain' was a dangerous job The air battles overhead, would not be heard as the tractor engine would completely drown it, and the drivers eye would be on the next cut, He most times only knew of the 'dog fight' overhead when he saw the vapour trails in the air, and the spitfires diving on the enemy aircraft. He was extremely vulnerable, he could be machine gunned by thr Germans or hit by a stray cannon shell as his trailer was last week.

When the spitfire dived on the enemy aircraft with its machine guns and cannons blazing away, it was inevitable that some of this fire had to hit the ground below, and so in this situation it was best to stop the tractor and get under it. Very little was written about the farm worker but he was an essential part of our war effort, keeping us in food. The only farm workers to get recognition were of course the land girls for obvious reasons.

Brother Ern was still at the printing works, this also was an important job, as there was a great deal on which we had to be informed There were posters eveywhere like 'careless talk costs lives,' 'don't be a rumour monger,' 'dig for victory and Britain,' and now and again morale boosters, like song sheets, with 'there will always be an England' ,and one that would bring tears to the eyes. Aimed at the children of soldiers, sailors, and airmen "goodnight children every where, your daddy thinks of you tonight, lay your head upon your pillow, don't be like a weeping willow, close your eyes and say a prayer, and surly you can find a kiss to spare, goodnight children everywhere"

The Germans had their propagander machine, but we had to try and keep our morale up, when we had very little to shout about.

Brother Les is still baking the bread from the wheat that Bill and Herby have grown, another importatant job. Unfortunately our two ounces of butter per week, has to be spread a little thinly. and our eight ounces of sugar does not let us make much jam, Wherever you went and whatever happened, nobody was in any doubt, we would win no matter how long it took.

At the moment we are getting a hell of a boost. The Germans are sending large numbers of aircraft against us, hundreds of them, and our spitfires and hurricanes are eating them up.

If you happen to be a small boy of 13 years looking up into a clear blue sky, listening to the rattle of machine guns, the enemy planes weaving about trying to avoid the firing, the sky full of vapour trails and the climax of a Gerry going down. Then this as Churchill said "was our finest hour"!

We have heard that one of these 'Gerrys' had been shot down, and is in a field at Kennington, and so that is where we are off to today not far on our bikes, just a couple of miles. Our objective was to get pieces off it, for our collection, to go with our bomb shrapnel, and bullets, and so when we arrived at the scene near Church Road, and saw this rather large bomber we thought we were in clover. As we approached a loud shout rang out "Halt"! move away from the area you boys. The RAF had placed two sentries to see nobody went near it, but they looked like a pair of decent guys who might respond to a bit of cheek, and we soon had a bit of banter going on. They did explain that nobody must go near it, until the men from the 'Ministry of Aircraft Production' had inspected it, as there could be something new on it that the 'Air Ministry' would want to see. But all we want we said was a piece of Perspex wind screen, and there is some under that wing. "right" they said take a piece and shove off! and we were gone.

Well we have cut it into squares, bevelled it, sand papered it, drilled and polished it, but our artistic flair has not yet shown up and so today we are going fishing. We have not made an early start today as we are going down the Marsh to the canal and as we have no fishing licence we have to avoid the gate keeper. His normal routine is to check the early birds, the real fishing experts, and then go home for his breakfast, and so we figure he is unlikely to leave his egg and bacon, when he later sees us some distance down the towpath.

Any way, off we go on our bikes, destination Hamstreet, via Kingsnorth Road. We had not been on the road long when a tractor and trailer came up behind and a loud voice "suggested", we move over we were somewhat surprised to find the driver was my brother Bill. He worked at Park Farm Kingsnorth, and lived in a small cottage by a moat, very picturesque, but it has all gone now for a housing estate. He is off down the Marsh to bring back a load of wheat, to be stacked at Park Farm, for thrashing later. "Where are you off too he asks? does mum know? "Oh get up on the back then, but don't tell mum I gave you a lift" Drop us up there a bit Bill, not too near the keepers cottage, off we got "thanks Bill". Off he went laughing, a little disturbing as his laugh could be heard for some distance. We went through the gate, along the hedge. and down to the canal, we could still be seen from the cottage, but we thought it rather unlikely that he would leave his breakfast for us.

We soon had our lines in the water, and with great expectations, had our eyes firmly on our floats. This is how it remained for the next hour, not even a 'bite', at this point my interest usually seems to wane and I lie back in the sun and hope my mates will tell me if I have a 'bite'. But a short while ago we heard the air raid sirens sound down the coast, and although it does not always mean an air raid, I thought I would just sit this one out.

This was no false alarm! There on the horizon were hundreds of dark shapes coming towards us with that unmistakable drone of engine noise. The excitement of a boys war, is draining away rapidly this was a terrifying sight, and the roar was getting closer.

Our only defence was the willow trees along the bank, with their wide trunks they would withstand stray bullets from above, but cannon shells from Spitfires we were not so sure.

Our situation has just got a little worse, down the towpath we can see the keeper heading our way at rather a fast pace. We are busy discussing whether we should face the Germans, or the gate keeper when Ray says "look" and there was the keeper looking skywards, but not for long, he was in his fifties, but he was sure racing for home. Now it did cross our minds that perhaps we should join him, but out of the frying pan, into the fire, did not seem a good idea at all. We knew of course that these large numbers of enemy aircraft would not break formation unless they came under attack. This meant that the if the RAF did not appear then they would just pass over us and continue on their way to London, and the unfortunate Londoners.

The rattle of machine guns tells us that the Spitfires have indeed arrived, and so there is no other option open to us, we now each have a three feet diameter willow trunk between us and the German Air Force.

The Spits will dive from above and will pick a target from that mass of aircraft, The bomber receiving the machine gun and cannon fire up his rear end, would decide perhaps he could shake off his attacker, and break formation. But his fate was usually sealed, as the Spitfire followed him down, still firing until the Gerry hit the ground, and burst into flames.

A cheer would go up from all around. Not a thought for the men burning in that plane, as by now we did not care how many Germans died, as long as they died, this feeling of hatred and loathing would take many years to die.

Three bombers have gone down, and the battle has gone by, many more will be shot down before they reach their target London. The danger for Ashford, is that when the Germans are being fired on by our Spitfires and Hurricanes, they will drop their bombs anywhere, in their bid to escape.

Well the 'all clear' is sounding along the coast, but we seem to have lost our interest in fishing, we are going home, this has scared the pants off us, and it will be a day we shall not forget.

On reaching home, I would have liked to have related what had happened, but mum would have hit the roof, but I was sure glad to get some food, mum always made sure of that.

Bill came home well into the evening and proceeded to tell the family what had taken place down the Marsh. During his account

Huckleberry Hawn

of the action he would have a sly grin at me and mum seemed to be putting two and two together, but if she did suspect anything, well she did not ask. Well that was pretty scary, but today we are roaming ROUND looking for something to do which up to now has not been very productive. The suggestion for tomorrow seems quite good, Saturday morning at the Odeon, just one snag, a little short of cash. Ray thinks that this might be overcome by another dig in my back garden, where we found all those coins before, being a super optimist, he had overlooked the fact that it had been dug many times before.

Mum is up town shoping, and so it is worth a go. Down our alley and through the back gate, and there we saw a rather worried man with his back against the fence and 'Tinker' our collie cross dog, with one paw either side of the mans face and looking the man straight in the eyes. The sight of this terrified man pleading for us to "call him off" just made us roll up with laughter, we thought it absolutly hilarious, and it was some minutes before we did as the man had asked, even if somewhat reluctantly. He then informed us that he was from 'RAF accounts' and demanded to see mum, we said he couldn't she was out, and so with a few grunts and a threat to tell mum, off he went.

Every year a man comes around to make sure dads dependants are not being overpaid, and that the family is as declared on mum's pay book. They need not have bothered, mum was the type that would never be dishonest, she was as straight as a dye, but that was one of the best laughs we had had for ages, serves him right!

Well we dug the garden again, but it had lone since given up its last sixpence, and after levelling it we decided on alternative entertainment.

A bomb had fallen about half a mile away in a field, and we are going to look for 'shrapnel'. this is what is left of the exploding bomb case. Most of the bomb would be flying in all directions, but as it was soft earth some would be in the bomb crater. We spent most of the morning digging ,and managed to find three pieces, each piece roughly about four inched long, about one and a half inches wide, and about half an inch thick, with an extremely jagged edge where it had been torn apart by the explosion. Each piece would have torn a terrible wound in its victim, an awful thought.

Well as much as I like the fun I have with Ray and Steve, today I am taking Tinker our collie for a nice walk over the Warren. It is quite early only 8.30, a lovely sunny morning again and with a bit of luck, I will be home before the Gerry bombers arrive, they seem to come later in the day, perhaps they have difficulty getting up. So I take hold of Tinkers lead, he goes berserk, and its off we go along Black Huts, Forge Lane, New Street, Magazine Road and onto the path leading to Warren Lane. This is a very pleasant walk, on our left we have the County School for girls (now Highworth) and on our right is this large field, mostly used for a very nice herd of dairy cows. Another occupant is the Skylark hovering high in the air, one would always hear them singing for all they are worth, while their partner sat on the nest down below, keeping an eye on the hoofs of the cows. A little dangerous. but in those days there seemed plenty of Skylarks, and so one would assume there were not too many casualties. A little further along the path there was a rather large object in the field opposite, which has nothing to do with agriculture, it is an anti aircraft gun emplacement. The 'gun crew' are enjoying a mug of tea, and a look at the paper, it was good to see them relaxing in the sun. They will be busy enough before the day is finished. We exchanged a few words, have a few laughs, they seemed a happy bunch, and I go on my way, I thought perhaps they had boys at home. They seemed to know boys.

Down the steps into Warren lane for a while, up the hill past the Isolation hospital of infectious diseases, and into the Warren. Tinker is off to explore every smell and every rabbit hole. Me I just love the absolute quiet, hardly a sound. No motorway noise no continuous procession of aircraft overhead, (well not yet anyway) just the sound of birds, woodpeckers, blackbirds, thrushes and many more, and perhaps the rustle in the ferns made by another dog and owner,

I made my way across the path ,until I came to a seat, by a large oak tree, it overlooks a mass of green ferns, and in the distance is the school, and the gun crew still enjoying the sun. I shall not sit here too long, as lovely as it is, as I would like to get back before any Gerry bombers appear. We know the Germans are not interested in Ashford when they send three or four hundred aircraft, we know they will hold formation until they are under sustained attack, but it is then that they will release their bombs, and make a run for it, though they seldom escape. These bombs will fall somewhere, and so it is best to be near some kind of shelter.

Well I think I am a bit late, I can hear the air raid sirens in Ashford and so I think I will stay where I am, I am not quite sure what route they will take, I may be well away from them.

I reckon this old oak will stop anything that might come my way. I can see them now, they darken the lovely blue sky, but they are about a mile away and so even if they jettison their bombs I shall not be in their path.

The gun crew are already in position, and with other crews in the area are putting up everything they have got, the noise is deafening they will continue firing unless the RAF are getting close, they obviously would not want to hit our own aircraft. Now instead of the loud crack of the AA guns there is the purr of the spitfires machine guns, but this time the bombers are accompanied by fighter planes, and the sky is a mass of vapour trails, as fighter takes on fighter. One is going down, but from this distance I cannot see if it is a Gerry or one of ours. The bombers are not getting away with it, they have lost one, and another is trailing smoke, and they still have a long way to go.

They cannot keep these losses up indefinitely, we are just into September,, and the RAF says that the Gerry's have lost 500 aircraft already, one has to bear in mind that is also 5oo aircrew. Well they are droning off into the distance, no danger to us, but certainly a danger to people between us and London, but if Hitler thinks he will break the spirit of the Londoner, he is quite mistaken.

The birds have begun to sing again, the sun is still shining the trails in the sky are disappearing all is nearly quiet on the South East front. I am tempted to make a move, but there has been no 'all clear' sounded in Ashford and I notice that the gun crew are still in their firing positions, and so I think I'll give it another few minutes maybe they know something I don't.

Tinker who has been curled up with me at the base of this large oak tree is getting up for another search of the area, he has been on the lead in case he ran off in terror, and I might not be able to find him. It is incredible, we have gone from war to peace in half an hour. The scene is the same as when I arrived, but I cannot soak it up now, as I did earlier, I feel that it will all start again, and Tinker and I will shake again at the base of this old oak.

The gun crew have turned their gun around it is now pointed in our direction, and behind me I can just hear the sound of aircraft. It sounds distinctly like a Gerry, they seem to have a different sound, I cannot see it, as behind me there is a bank of trees, hopefully the pilot will want to clear these trees (and me) It is coming over now, it is a Gerry with smoke coming from one engine, much lower than I am sure that he would like to be, but that engine is obviously no use now, I think his chances are pretty slim. The gun crew are now having a go, although I don't think their shells are any good against an aircraft at that height, unless they get a direct hit. Other guns are joining in now, his chances are reducing by the minute, he is going down, no one has bailed out, it hits the ground about two miles away in a field and bursts into flames, Whether this gun crew got it is debatable but they are going to claim it I guess, along with several other crews.

Well that's it !I am going home regardless, we have sat by this old oak for long enough, I think Tinker has also had enough, and is happy to go. We walk a bit faster through the ferns, into the lane, up the steps and along the path towards the gun. As we approach we get a cheer from the crew, not for anything we had done, but just because they had done what they were trained to do, and their unit would claim the 'kill'. How was that mate! did you see it? Yes I said, congratulations, hoping their pride was justified. The whole crew just had to tell me how they did it. Well you had better get off home now before it starts again son, and that was just what I had in mind.

Passing along the path the skylarks were singing again, the cows were munching grass, all was well and I would soon be home.

I got to thinking about that German air crew, and all that would remain of them, just the fireproof tags they wore around their necks for identification so that the relatives could be told your son/husband/father has been killed in action. I thought of the boy like me ,who would never see his father again, who would never fish in the river with dad, never fly a kite with dad, never picnic with mum and dad in the forest, and it seemed so sad.

Hang on! hang on mate! they were only Germans! said a voice from within, yes of course, sorry, I guess for a moment I thought they were people, the voice from within brought me back to earth, and I quickened my pace, and on to Magazine Road, New Street, Forge Lane, Black huts and a sight for sore eyes. My house where mum would be.

Mum asked me where I had been when the Gerry's came over, and I said I was quite safe where I was, and she accepted that. It was after all not possible to stay indoors all the time, daily life had to go on. The air raid siren sounded usually in good time and it was up to the individual to take over quickly.

Well several days have passed since my walk with Tinker to the Warren and seeing the 'Gerry' go down, and burst into flames on hitting the ground, but I keep thinking about the way I was concerned about that German air crew, possibly burnt alive.

This crew might well have been involved in the merciless blitz on Warsaw, Rotterdam, London and many more. They would possibly be responsible for torn bodies, bodies buried under tons of masonry, people burned alive just as they were, so why should I be concerned? I thought too of that gun crew, perhaps one of them was a Londoner, he would see this mass of enemy bombers coming towards him. He would not have time to think then, his job as part of the team was to keep slamming those shells into that gun, but once the action was over, he would know those bombers were heading for the city where we lived, perhaps to the very road where his family were, and he would want to go to them, but he could not. He would also know that even if he was able to get to them, it would not be long before the 'Military Police' would be knocking on his door, to arrest him for being 'absent without leave'. He would be taken back to his unit and charged. He would then be subject to the strictest discipline. Possibly in a special camp where the 'jailers' would take great delight, in trying to break him so that he would have no inclination to return, it was invariably successful.

I have thought a great deal about my concern for the enemy, and have decided to do as my teacher says" (must try harder) I must hate a little more, and I think before this is all over, this will come very easily.

Brother Ernest has been reading the 'dig for victory 'posters and has decided an allotment on a piece of ground owned by his employer might be a good idea. Much of the vegetables sold in the South East go first to 'Convent Garden' London, a very large fruit and veg market. Obviously life in London is a little uncertain, and so an allotment with a few vegetables would be a good standby.

I am second in command, and it being Saturday afternoon we are doing our bit, and getting a few spuds out of the ground, or we were, shall I say, I don't think much more will be done as cousin

Huckleberry Hawn

Monty has arrived. Monty does not come down here to help, he only comes to 'stir things up' take the Micky, or in other words. have a jolly good laugh, but in these days that is no bad thing, laughs are a little hard to come by.

Saturday night is bath night, and tonight is the night, a couple of hours ago we began the operation, by lighting the copper This was a large copper tub with a fire grate below it, and old rubbish would burn on this and would produce enough hot water for a bath for the four youngest. The older ones would go to the bath house, in Elwick Road.

The water is now hot, next we bring in the tin bath, which we keep in the shed. Having put the hot water in the bath, the first body is ready. This is Rita, our sister gets first bath, not so much for 'ladies first' but because in t hose days neither sex were supposed to know what was under the cloths of the opposite sex. The only good thing about this I think was that the population grew a little less rapidly than today.

After Rita, a rapid conveyor type system, soon had us three boys spotlessly clean. thoroughly scrubbed with 'Lifebouy' soap, not highly scented, but mum would say, a good clean smell. After bath time there was emptying down the drain, and generally cleaning up.

How nice it is today, to pull the plug and it just drains away. All this activity has taken place in the 'scullery' a room that today would be called the kitchen, the copper is in the corner of the room, along with this was the 'kitchener'. This was a cast iron stove which would have pans on top. and an oven by the side. It was a must that it really shone, the shine was produced by much rubbing with 'black lead' like a sort of black shoe polish.

Monday morning the scullary will again be the centre of much activity, when all the cloths of the family will be placed in the copper probably with a liberal amount of 'Rinso' washing powder, and boiled. Then to the sink to drain. and out to the monster in the yard, this was a cast iron frame about five feet high with two rollers made of wood about seven inches in diameter Fortunately mum was a tough old bird, so she found little difficulty in feeding the clothing through, and at the same time turning the handle.

It is quite a good idea to be somewhere else on Mondays, and today I am off to school. My Monday morning feeling is a little easier to bear whenI think of the 'sparks' flying at home. I was less happy with Monday, because the first lesson was with teacher Nixone we have a sort of mutual respect for each other, but now we are with Mr Battle for maths, not my favourite lesson. but he was a nice guy. The lesson however must be interrupted as the air raid siren has gone, and we must all make our way, as quickly as we can to the air raid shelters. We usually had time with a good fast walk to get there before the Gerry's.

The shelters are just brick buildings, about eight feet high, with a twelve inch deep slab of concrete on top, not much good if a bomb is close. Inside the light is very poor, not much good for lessons, but in order to keep us quiet Mr Battle has devised a game that each pair of boys can play, We each have a four inch square of paper, on which are a number of small squares. In three of these we put, B.C.D. for battleship, cruiser, destroyer i'll say to the other ?? I fire my guns into B square, the other boy has to show him if he was on target, Unfortunately my opponent is not co-operating, and so I have had to give him a little persuasion, during which his 'ouch" was heard by the master, and we were invited to see him after school. Strangely enough, I was not able to keep this appointment due to the appearance of the 'Gerrys'.

We had been on one of our trips of the local industries, this particular one was the local Electricity Generating Plant in Victoria Road, (no longher in use). It was very interesting seeing these huge engins, they seemed enormous, with ear shattering noise, and I thought of them running day and night, with the engineer standing by them, and the town depending on the electricity produced, this trip was good. On the way home, which took us across Victoria Park on our way to the school, the air raid siren was sounded, we were at this point just passing the 'band stand' where the local band would play on Sunday afternoons, and below which was an air raid shelter. It was almost time to go home from school, but no chance of that now. However it was not all bad, firstly I would not have to keep my appointment with the teacher, for my little disagreemant with my fellow pupil, and secondly because the ladies living in the road nearby, 'Hillbrow Road, had heard about the poor little boys in the shelter, and they were bringing us all sorts of goodies. They were so nice, just like mums everywhere.

The Gerry's have increased their activity to cover a much wider area, but are paying a very high price, the latest one day count, was probable 185, definite 56, general opinion is they cant keep this up much longer.

It's Sunday morning ,and I am off down the allotment to get some vegetables for dinner, because it is quite early there is not much moving, Sunday morning 'lie ins' were more the thing in those days. Very little sport, no boot fairs, no hi-fi, just people going to church, all seemed well with the world. Above me I could see a lone Spitfire, it was flying perfectly well, no variation in its course, the engine sounded fine as it purred along, it was good to see one of our fighter pilots just coasting home, having probably just left a battle. What happened next will stay with me always, With its engine still running perfectly, not a sound of a splutter or bang, it just went into a vertical dive, I followed it down until I heard the crash. I have never known just what happened to that gallant pilot, but I thought a lot about him. I have a picture of this Spitfire being involve in an air battle some where over the channel, where I am sure he would have put up a damned good show, but he probably was severely wounded, and although his plane still flew, he could no longer fight, He turned for home desperately hoping his strength would hold, just long enough to put his plane down on the nearest airfield, but it was not to be. I think he just died at the controls, his body fell forward and he and his Spitfire fell to earth, the land of his birth.

He would obviously have been one of the country's best. He would have been to Cranwell, learnt to fly, proudly put his 'wings' on his RAF uniform. His parents would have come to his 'passing out parade, full of pride, mingled with fear, but no sign of the fear would show. This was his day, there may be very few left. Now there will be just a few photos on the sideboard, and the memories of the last 21 years.

Now I think I have learned too hate.

Off to school today, and I'll bet because I would love to see the 'Gerry's' today they will not turn up. The reason I would like to see t hem is that the first lesson is the one I hate, it is art. An air raid warning would mean a very swift move to the air raid shelters, and the end of my art lesson. The only rotten thing about it was that the teacher giving the lesson at the time of the warning. must remain with the class. I think Mr Sarcro and I, had a sort of mutual loathing. He seemed to be able to read my mind, and know just what I was thinking of him. I despised him because he was only interested in the one third of the class that showed any sign of artistic promise. It was obvious that the other two thirds would not be likely to copy the 'Mona Lisa', or Constables Haywain, Although if there was, I think being the true Scot from North of the border that he was, the financial aspect would have made him see us in an entirely different light.. Well no air raid warning and so on to maths with **Mr Battle** it was not my favourite lesson but Mr Battle knew how to teach and he had what I have always demanded from a person, a smile. He would crouch down beside our desks, and with a smile, tell us where we were going wrong, not in a fast, sarcastic way, but quite slowly so that we always got the point. He taught the 'A' stream. and our reports were usually quite good. No air raid warning. So it is on to Moggy Horgan, not many smiles here, but he knows his subject, and as geography is my favourite, we get on quite well. He is a rather short man, and a little round, but if we work well, we get on well. Still no air raid warning, and onto our last lesson. Its english with Nixone, he and I have crossed swords a few times, but while I have loathing for my art master, I have respect for Nixone, and I think he would say the same about me. He is very strict, but good at his job, and because of this, he expects absolute commitment and will tolerate no pranks in his lesson, as I have found out in the past!

We have managed a full mornings schooling, and no sign of the Gerry's. I am pleased that we have ,as I am in my forth year, next year I shall be 14 years old, and will be leaving to start work, what I will do will depend on what is on offer at the time.

Its been a great summer 'weather wise', but it is getting a little cool in the evenings, and this we have noticed, has meant smoke coming from some of the chimneys. This of course means our fire lighting bobbins will again be in demand, and so after school tomorrow we shall be going to the market to get our supplies. There are two fruit and veg stalls with nice guys, but they seem to take a great dislike to us. It's the apple and orange boxes we are after, as they are made of quite thick wood and will chop up nicely. The stalls are arranged in an oval shape, and the customers are not supposed to get into the area behind the stalls as the stall holders always suspect something might go missing. Fortunately her little farm, and next to her is a guy demonstrating household gimmics, like tin openers of knife sharpeners, etc, and so neither of them are too concerned when we slip through. We casually saunter up to the back of this stall, and have each picked up two nice boxes, enough for a couple of dozen bobbins. As we turn to go an ear shattering voice bawls out, Git art of it ya little brats. least I think it was brats, it began with a B. This loosely translated meant, would you boys mind leaving the area around my stall please. However there was a definite sense of urgency in the gentleman's voice, which needed acting on immediately, and we were off heading for the gap where we knew we could escape, once out of the market we did not have far to go.

Most of the stall holders came from London and were really not bad guys, after all just living in London was no picnic. Most of our fruit boxes would come from the whoesale market at Covent Garden, all this had to be done with the possability of German air raids. Not bad guys ,they just had a healthy suspicion of small boys. Between now and the weekend we shall chop up our boxes and should end up with plenty of bobbins, and a 7 for six pence will supply us with enough cash for our seats at the Odeon Saturday morning. It costs 3 pence each to go to the Odeon but with a bit of luck, one ticket will get all three of us into the Cinema in Beaver Road, t hat's if they have not locked the back door.

At school today my feelings for Sarcro the art master deteriorated a little further. We had just finished a special science lesson, which had over run a little, it is not a lesson where one can be that precise, Unfortunately the next lesson was with Nixone for English, and we all knew Nixone demanded punctuality. This we thought necessitated a gentle trot along the corridor although anything but walking was extremely forbidden. We were moving along at a nice pace, by no means running, when the last person we wanted to see was coming up the steps at the other end. Sarcro was not a lot over five feet tall with a face so red and lined that you might think he had spent his life as a highland farmer, perhaps he had. There he was coming over the top looking for all the world like gnome without a hat, or perhaps Sherpa Tensing coming over the summit of Everest. Raising himself up to his full height, he said in the loudest voice he could manage, "stop"! This order had to be obeyed or it would be another visit to the headmaster Willy Pumphrene something I was getting better at avoiding. "Fetch my strap Jones" and Jones went off at walking speed, but I am sure when he was out of sight, he managed a little trot, as Sarcro was a rather impatient man. When Jones came back with the strap, which ironically he was also about to partake, we were made to line up with our hand out stretched one hand under the other. This meant the hand to take the punishment did not move so much, and therefore the impact was greater, and the pain likewise. In those days we were brought up to take our punishment without question, but I think today Sarcro would probably be found with that strap wound tightly around his more tender parts, possibly with Ray and me at each end of the strap. The first phase of the battle of Britain is now drawing to a close, the Germans daylight raids have been very costly, the RAF estimates the Germans probably losses at 2692 aircraft, and their commandant Goering has been forced to change his tactics. This has meant more night raids, I would much rather see the swines, than just hear them, and I am sure the London people are not too pleased It means as many as possible crowd into the tube tunnel to sleep, they are quite safe there but the conditions must have left a great deal to be desired. In the morning they would come up to the surface, and hurry to their homes, but some would only find a mound of rubble, or smouldering timbers. They would be taken to temporary accommodation by caring people like the 'Church army' or 'Salvation army' while they mourned the loss of so much they held so dear. But you would never hear any suggestion of surrender quite the opposite, it would not be many days before they would be more determined than ever. The German's idea that they could break the spirit of the people would never happen, one speech by Churchill, and it was, lets get at them!

Back home in Ashford we would have gone to bed nice and warm, and fast asleep, but the air raid sirens have sounded, and mum has done what we have been told to do, get in the safest part of the house which is the cupboard under the stairs. She will have taken the youngest, and she will be calling up the stairs to the rest of us, "The air raid sirens have sounded, are you coming down?" "Yes we will be down in a moment" a few minutes later she would call again, and get the same reply, but after two or three tries she would leave us to it, she had done all she could.

She would now tap on the wall, and call out to the neighbours who were getting on in years, I don't know if it was for the neighbours, or just to reassure herself. Anyway it did both a lot of good, just to know you were not alone was everything. Looking back on it ,it was probably not as safe as we thought, nestling in there with mum, was the gas meter.

I think the thing I most longed for was an unbroken nights sleep, for although we had not had the bombing of some citys, it was the nightly sound of the sirens, and the ear shattering sound of Anti aircraft fire, that woke us most nights. Although mum could not get us out of our beds, it was not possible to sleep. The drone of the Gerry's we knew should not be of much risk to us, they were mostly heading for London, but when the search lights picked them out, and the A A fire got too close, they might just unload their bombs anywhere. Daylight would come ,and it would be off to school or work, life had to go on, England expected every man to do his duty!

September the anniversary month of the outbreak of war has now gone, the first phase of the battle of Britain has been won. Losses in enemy aircraft are put at 2692 probably destroyed, but 1733 aircraft were definitely shot down, This victory was very much needed, but it was achieved at awful losses to our young pilots, in the RAF, some of them would be only 6 years older than me.

Churchill's words "never was so much owed by so many to so few" will always bring back the memory of twelve spitfires diving on a mass of German aircraft, that was usually the number at any one time. Imagine the feelings of these pilots, the odds were stacked against them, but in they went, and the enemy losses speak forthemselves.

Field Marshal Herman Goering, the big fat German in charge of the German aircraft, would now be standing in front of Hitler. The Fuhrer would be ranting, and raving, demanding an explanation, how could these little Englanders defeat his arial

armada. Goering would give all kinds of reasons, but one reason he could not give was that the bravery of those spitfire
and hurricane pilots tore the heart out of that armada.

The RAF, which now has many pilots from around the world must carry on, but they have given us a much needed victory, there has not been much to cheer about on land or sea, and Churchill again adds a few most impressive words:
"If the British Empire lasts for a thousand years, men will still say, THIS was their finest hour!."

It is October now and every year at this time its chestnutting. Today it is down to the drive on our bikes usually with a good stick which we throw up into the tree, but this year I have come up with another idea, I have tied the stick to a length of string. When the stick lodges up in the branches I pull and shake the branch, and down come the nuts, works a treat. A man standing watching us said "that boy will go far", well I did, but no tin the way he meant, I went to Palestine as a soldier, I became a first rate 'tradesman', but neither of which made me rich, well not in money. But in life in general, I can't complain, as the old saying goes, you can't win them all!

The nuts usually ended up being roasted under the coal fire, after they have been pricked with a fork. However tonight I am receiving black looks from father as one has just exploded with a loud bang, I guess I failed to prick that one, he probably thought he was being shot at.

Today I am doing my bit for food production, there is a rabbit problem on the farm, and Bill and his mate Dave are going to catch a few. Dave has a ferret and nets, the plan is to put the nets over the smaller burrows, and the ferret down the main burrow. Bill will be at the netted entrance to one hole, and I will be at one. The rabbits seeing the ferret will quickly make for an escape hole, and Bill and I will catch t hem in the nets. Well it seemed simple enough, but my end did not go as planned, the rabbits came to the surface, and Bill and Dave quickly "dispatched" theirs, but I just could not bring myself to kill mine, and Dave had to do mine as well. I think they both understood, and did not really expect a thirteen year old to kill an animal as they would. They were however quite happy with the afternoons work. Twenty three rabbits, less to eat the cabbage plants, this was good for the farm. The rabbits would be very useful to us, in helping the meat ration further. The meat ration was half a pound, per week, and for a manual worker like Bill, it was not really enough, at least that was what mum felt, and so the rabbits would be a useful addition to our meat ration. Most of all though ,it meant that I would get the skins ,and I would be off up Forge Lane to the 'rag and bone' man, who would pay three pence per skin. This was why I had really volunteered to help in the operation, well also for the country's food production of course!

Mum is a little upset this evening, Ernest, her number two son, has said that he is thinking of volunteering for the RAF. She knows in the back of her mind that if the war goes on long enough, all her sons will be taken from her, and I think she feels that when they are "called up" that will be soon enough.

All men of eighteen years of age and over are being 'called up' for the services, army, navy or RAF. There are few exceptions only 'conscientious objectors', mainly on relgious grounds, or 'reserved occupations', Bill is in the last category, as he is engaged in food production, very important in our situation as an island.

Erne says that he does not want to be shoved into the army, or navy, he says that it is inevitable that before long his turn will come, and he would rather be in the RAF like dad.

This did not go down well with mum, she quickly pointed out that if dad had not volunteered, he would have probably not gone at all, and she would not be in the position she is in now. Well that sort of killed the discussion stone dead. It was not that mum was without any feeling of patriotism, she was a mum, and she knew how many young men had died already. The thought of losing all her sons was more than she could bear, and she put on her coat and hat, and said she was taking the dog for a walk. Rita said she would come with her, but mum said "no thanks love" and Rita k-new better than to insist. That was a few days ago, and Ern has mum on her own, and so has taken the opportunity of putting his case again.

Look mum I know how you must feel, but I am going to be called up sooner or later, it can't be long now. John and Sid have been called up for the army, they did not mind which service they joined, but I would like to join the RAF as a photographer, and soon I could be too late, I too could be placed in the army. There was a long silence, and then in a very soft voice she said, "Ernest, I have had eight children seven of them sons, I know that by the end of the war I may have none!" I cannot hand them to the war office willingly, equally I know I cannot hold onto them, the government will get them one by one, until they have them all. "I know you think you know how I feel, but only a woman, and mother could know that, but I do know how you feel son, and you must do what you as a man in time of war must do". All I can do is pray the Lord goes with you. "Go ahead son, and I hope it is the RAF, and not the army.

Ern was so relieved, he did not want to hurt mum, but he wanted to get on with that which he knew was inevitable. He has now volunteered, and is due to go before a medical board, to see if he has any medical problems, in a fortnights time.

It is November 5th, Guy Fawks night, we don't have fireworks, and of course can't have a bonfire in case The Gerrys see it, but we still go round with our 'guy' in the pram. A pair of old trousers and shirt stuffed with anything we can lay our hands on and chat people up for a 'penny for the guy' most people laugh at our cheek and toss us a coin, "thanks mister"!

It was one of two nights in the year when we were VIPs, we take our takings to Hansons fish and chip shop, order our fish and chips and sit in the restaurant, The lady would bring it in and we would sure enjoy it. She had a beaming smile on her face, seeing three cheeky boys living it up, and I don't think she really expected a tip, as she still had a grin when we left.

When I arrived home mum was still rather cross, she had had a few words with the 'air raid warden' He had been a chink of light showing through the black curtains. When the light was on in the room we had to make sure no light could be seen from outside, in case the Gerrys saw it. It was not a nice situation, the whole town in complete darkness. Tonight it happens to be the young a warden, a right 'little Hitler', he would shout "you are showing a light, cover it, as he banged the door, I think he knew better than to hang around, brother Les would wring his neck.

The older wardens were so different, they would knock and say "excuse me, but do you know you are showing a light", and of course we woudl soon find the problem, and say "sorry about that", and there would be no bad feelings. We had to be very careful about lights, even the headlights on lorrys were blacked out except for a slit about 2 inches deep across the lamp.

Mum is a little quiet these days, Ern passed his medical and is now at an RAF camp in Bedfordshire, he is very pleased as he has got what he wanted, he is now a trainee photographer. I think having a father in the RAF, also a photographer helped a bit.

Things are a bit quiet all round at home. Billy who normally has plenty of things to say, seems somewhat subdued. Perhaps it is because his brother, two years younger than himself has volunteered for service, and he will not be called up as he is in reserved occupation. He is a skilled farm worker, and food production is an absolute priority.

The young men of the area were being called up quite rapidly, and any one of military age who did not seem to go, uaually received rather nasty looks. Of course the neighbours would not dare say any thing to mum, they knew she hated nosy people, and she would flatten them.

Dad gets home most weekends, and as long as he is back in camp by 1 minute to midnight Sunday nights he is ok. Ern is not quite so lucky, he will not be allowed out of camp, until he has completed his basic training, with special care to make sure he wears his uniform properly, looks smart and is a credit to his unit. Most of all, he must be able to give a good salute to any officer he may meet. Ern would have no difficulty here, as Bill, Ern and Les would have had behaviour and respect drummed into them by mum, she as a young mum, would have considered this as an absolute must, I think however as her large family came along, she had less, and less, time to impress this on the rest of us, I was no 5, and there were three more yet to come, but even so, she still expected us to show respect to most grown ups.

I had a little difficulty when my turn came to join the army, where this was concerned, as while I could respect any man officer or otherwise, I demanded this respect be returned, and in the army there were little 'Hitlers', with one, two or three stripes on their arms, As I stared them straight in the eyes, I remembered those words, 'All power corrupts, absolute power corrupts absolutely" and those other immortal words, 'Never let the baskets see they've got you' but that's another story.

I shall learn a lot about life in the next four years, before I am eighteen, and of call up age.

London is still taking a pounding from the Gerry's mostly by night now, we get the news of an awful night on the radio, but of course we only see the pictures of the fires and destruction when we go to the Cinema. The destruction is of course still supposed to bring us to our knees, but by the look of the Londoner amid his shattered home, there is very little chance of that! Other cities are being subjected to the same treatment, Hitler still thinks we will break and he will be able to just walk in, but it only has the reverse effect. One of the worst attacks has been made on Coventry, very many have died, and much of the city distsroyed, including the beautiful cathedral, but our day will come!

Its been a quiet day today not much on the radio so I am off to bed, it is only ten o'clock but a good nights sleep is very acceptable, most of us are usually in bed by 10,30 anyway, it could also be a quiet night. No such luck, the sirens are sounding there is a rumble in the distance, and I can hear mum getting the two youngest out of bed. As she passes our door on her way to the cupboard, she quietly calls out, the sirens have gone, are you getting up? The reply is always the same, yes in a moment, but she knows that a warm bed will nearly always win. She calls so softly that you would think she was afraid the Gerry's would hear, but I think she always knew we would probably not be getting up, and so she really did not want to wake us right up. Tonight though there are five of us in the cupboard, as much as we would like to have stayedin our beds Reg and I have joined mum, now and again a couple of us keep her company, as the thought of her downstairs in that cold cupboard, hurts nearly as much as getting out of bed, usual ritual, she calls the neighbours through the wall, just a few words to reassure them, and herself then we just sit and listen to the drone of the Gerry's above and the whacking great crack of the anti-aircraft guns.

We know that they have very little interest in Ashford, but if those search-lights pick them out, and the guns have their range, then the bombs could be anybodys.

If a bomb was to fall near our house and not actually on it we would probably be ok, as the staircase is quite often still in one piece, and so the cupboard under the stairs is the safest part of the house.

The drone above goes on, and we try to drift off, but it is pretty useless, I think if it was not for the A A guns I could. I look at young Rita close to mum I think of the line in the wartime song, "and Jimmy will go to sleep in his own little room again" and it cannot come soon enough, but this is only year two and we are still very much on the defensive, but not down hearted It's been a long night, it is almost 4 a m and the all clear is only just being sounded, we heave ourselves up and head for bed. Mum says anyone for a cup of tea, but there are no takers, we throw ourselves into bed, and hope the rest of the night is quiet.

Seven o/clock and time to get up, the older ones for work, the younger ones for school, nobody feels like it, but like robots we almost fall downstairs, life goes on, at least for the lucky ones. Its been another quiet day, it seems the RAF had made it uncomfortable for the Gerry's by day, they prefer not to be seen, it makes us feel helpless, we all do our bit but we cannot go on the offensive, we need much more in the way of aircraft and guns.

The man reading the news tells us of the invasion ships, being assembled across the chanel, and how the RAF "re-arranges" them each night and so tomorrow Ray, Steve and I think we will cycle down to the coast to see what our defences are like, it's only ten miles, On our way we notice the larger fields have sprouted 10 feet posts like tree trunks, these will stop any enemy gliders landing troops, obviously a good defensive idea, not much else, except the anti-aircraft guns and their neighbours the searchlight crews, they work together with good results, but when we reached the coast we let out a loud Gor-blimy! look at that barbed wire as far as you could see. This was not going to stop us getting down to the sea, or so we thought.

Ray and Steve tore off along the path, but as I looked out to sea through the wire, I thought about the rumor that large drums of petrol had been placed along the coast ready to be ignited should the Germans set foot on our beaches.

Always having a good imagination, I produced an invasion scene, German landing craft running onto the beach, troops stepping off into waist deep water, this would be a signal for the petrol to be poured onto the sea, a flare would then be fired into it AND the sea would be a mass of flames. The enemy soldiers would scream in agony as their clothing and hair began to burn. They would go below the water to escape but when they came up, it would be just the same, it seemed more and more went below the surface, but less and less came up.

Some would make a desperate dash to get out of the water, only to be killed by the machine gunners on the cliff top. Bodies piled up, and the cries from the sea grew less and less, the machine guns ceased firing and the flames were dying down. At this point my imagination produced a crowd of people from the bombed and burnt cities of Coventry and London, they were behind me and made hardly a sound, so awful was the sight before them, burning bodies of any nationality were a terrible sight.

Suddenly a rather learned voice spoke in a loud clear tone "This surely is a hidious example of mans inhumanity to man", but hardly had he stopped than a chorus of North country and cockney voices shouted, rot in hell you swines, rot in hell.

I don't think a word would have been said, the scene was so ghastly, but this cultured voice expressing concern, for soldiers of a nation which had bombed and burned children, wives, mums grand mums of my imaginary crowd behind was more than they could bear, To some degree the learned gentleman was right, but for the people of Britain, the Germans had long since forfieted all rights to any humanitarian considerations, not only were we suffering from their indiscriminate bombing but as yet we have not got the bombers ot hit back, but our day will come!

Ray and Steve are back, Watcha looking at? they ask, for a minute I was speechless, coming back to earth with a bump, they were also looking out to sea. I can't see anything, no I said, I thought I saw a submarine, but I guess not.

This discussion came to an abrupt end, as a loud nasty voice rang out, "you boys, this is a prohibited area, leave immediately" Well we had been brought up to respect our elders, but not when the tone of voice was like that, and so we were looking around for this bloke and we would give him a dose of his own medicine. "Now" came the voice again and looking round there on the beach behind the barbed wire was an Army Officer and two soldiers, the soldiers were holding a board, with a map or chart on it. The Officer looked decidedly trigger happy and so we did what any good soldier would do, obey the last order.

We did not need much persuading, there is not much here now, the ice cream huts are boarded up, no boats on the canal, hardly a soul in sight, a really uncanny experience.

Ray says the last one up the hill is a Nazi, and we are off at break neck speed, needless to say I was last, but I carry a little more weight than they do.

On arriving home mum asks the usual question, what have you been doing? she knows we have to go out, war or no war, but I think it makes her feel easier if she gets a reasuring reply, been looking for bomb craters mum, find any? yes, and a few bits of shrapnel (bomb case) great.

It was no good telling her where we had really been, she had enough on her plate without worrying herself un-necessarily about us. Ern of course is in the RAF, but she still has to control the other seven, the older ones are now fifteen, seventeen, and twenty one.

This evening there is a nasty difference of opinion between Les and Bill, Les has a rather short fuse, and will react quite decisivly to anything personal, he has just hurled a bottle of Tomato sauce at Bill, it has missed, and is not running down the wall, Les is a big fella, Bill not quite so big, but just as determined not to back down. This of course was what mum was so afraid of when dad went into the RAF, she knew she could never intervene in a situation like this, and the younger ones were just children, and would have very little chance against men like these.

Her only chance was to get the old chap accross the road He was a very frail man that a good wind would blow over, but Paddy would came across, and put his self between them.

What he said to them would never be heard, and so it was pointless to try, being an old man and rather thin I think he knew the boys would never harm him. Having calmed them down, he would appeal to them in his Irish voice to realise that their mother was in an awful situation, and she needed their support, don't you make it worse for her, boys he said, and what about your dad don't you think he would want you to look after her? not to scare her out of her wits. Now can I take it that you will give her no more trouble tonight? Yes, sorry Paddy it won't happen again, and Paddy shook hands with them and wispered to them "look after her now"

He went over to mum patted her on the shoulder and said I will be off now Violet, they will be alright now, right boys? and as they nodded their heads, he dragged his feet across the road to his house.

Paddy was a chimney sweep, he had a wife who organised his day for him. He would push his little barrow around town doing his job, but he had one failing, he would call in a public house or two for a drink, probably to wash the soot from his throat, but on this point, his wife and himself could never see eye to eye, I think she felt that in the drinking time he could have swept more chimneys.

It was not just the Germans, the air raids, the sleepless nights, it was the daily quarrels that affected mum most, with seven children there was always a dis-agreement of some sort, not of course like the one last night between Bill and Les, but her family, and the war meant she felt as if she was sitting on a volcano, any minute something could blow.

Some of the dis-agreements she would not tolerate, like the never ending moans about sugar rationing, where was it all going? Well in the end she gave the whole lot of us a jar with our half pound of sugar in it, even then there was the occasional suggestion that one or the others ration had been got at. Today she has given us a choice ,either we put half of our ration in her cooking jar, or she will make no effort to prepare a few goodies for christmas, of course everyone has agreed, without hesitation.

Mum will not be able to do a lot, most things are difficult to obtain. We have our ration books for Meat, Butter, Sugar etc. and there is another one of "points" this points book covers things in short supply, but not always available. If something became available up town, the news would spread like wild-fire Liptons have dried fruit,, Woolworths have chocolate, then its on the bike and off as fast as I can. Today we have managed to get some sultanas, so mum will make a cake, it won't be her usual christmas cake but that won't matter. She has some ginger wine essence which with sugar and water, will produce a reasonably nice drink, non-alcholic of course, we did not have wine or beer in the house, I don't know why, maybe it was money, or just that dad was not that keen, but if mum could accumalate a little spare sugar she would love to make her Cherry Brandy, and that was really nice.

The meat ration could be helped with the addition of a few Rabbits, and at christmas there is always a nice piece of pork for the men on the farm. This was really against the law as every animal slaughtered must be reported to the ministry of food, but of course there is a little fiddle in most things like food, so with meat and plenty of vegetables, fruit from the orchard, we shall have a reasonably good day. When we think of the victims of Hitler we have to feel exceedingly thankfull, and we do.

Dad should be home for christmas, and we hope Ern as well and so the family will be together, with the noise that a family of ten can make, Gran will not say much, she will just give us black looks if she disapproves of something, and she almost certainly will.

Well it has come once again, the second wartime christmas, Mum has worked so hard all day, she has hardly sat down, except for "THE KING". Now it is evening, and she is fast asleep in her easy chair. Worked hard she has, but the look of contentment on her face I have not seen for a long time. She has had all the family around her, plenty of laughs, and no German aircraft. Peace and quiet now, a feeling of being safe in her own home. The cupboard under the stairs will not be required tonight. It has been a rather noisy day inside, but the street out side has like most christmases been very quiet.

Only a very few people go out, it is a family occasion. It is quite quiet inside now, not just mum but some of the other members of the family seem to be nodding. I think what might have brought this sleepiness on was mums cherry brandy. She must have found it difficult with so little sugar available, but I think we all may have made a contribution from our sugar ration without us knowing it, it would possibly explain the difference in the sugar level in our jars, which we blamed on each other, still it was worth every grain.

The warm happy feeling it produced made christmas 1940 a very much deserved reward for us all, and when mum filled our glasses it was plain too see that sense of pride in her ability to produce this wonderful liquid that warmed the inside and put a smile on the outside. Ernie being the sort of speaker for the party decided to toast should be made, "TO THE END OF THE WAR", we all drank to that, dad not wishing to be out done proposed his toast, "that we all come through this safely and that I take the photo of my life, of us all at peace doing what we used to do before all this began".

Well this seemed to bring smiles all round, and so I thought I would join in, "TO MUM" she who inspires us all with her guts and determination, "unfortunately it did not have the effect I thought it would, mum's eyes began to water and it looked as if she would begin to cry, we could not let this happen, she was enjoying herself and this was something we did not see very often. She was quickly covered in the arms of her family nearest to her and given a big kiss from our sister Rita.

As a family we did not go in for a lot of affectionate displays, but Rita was a little more soft hearted than the boys and we were very pleased to see her do that, which I think we would all like to do ourselves, but have not got the nerve, our show of affection quickly brought her back and with a smile from ear to ear, she decided she must say a few words herself.

I don't have to tell any of you that life is at times just a little hard, I have asked myself sometimes ,can I go on, well after today I can safely say ,yes I can, for as long as it takes we will carry on, just bear with me now and again if I can't find much to make me smile, we all gave a loud cheer and another hug. Well like I said most of us were nodding now ,so I think I will lead the way up too bed, it is almost certain to be a quiet night as the Germans also like to celebrate christmas, so we all round off a lovely day with a good night's sleep, we could not ask for more, 'Happy Christmas!"

Fantastic, three good nights sleep, but the Germans who having also celebrated christmas and probably preached good will too all men are now doing just what they were doing before christmas bombing London and most of our big cities. London has had their worst fire bomb raid. The Gerry's have dropped thousands of phoshorus fire bombs, they are not that big, but as soon as they strike their target the phoshouus will ignite and be white hot in minutes soon setting fire to all around it .Water is not much use against phoshorus, it has to be a bucket of sand over it, but of course you have to see it land or hear it, but with all the noise going on, that was difficult, and so many of them did what they were intended to do and produced a blazing London.

The government have now ordered that all work places must have fire watchers on duty every night ,with containers of sand ready at hand. We shall not be caught by them again. How we would like to return their "goodwill", but the day will come.

We have not had much to shout about, but the RAF made it pretty plain to the Germans that they had better not come by day and now we are getting some good news from the Mediterranean area. The Navy is knocking hell out of the Italian Navy, it has now become clear why they built their Warships for speed, sometimes it is necessary to go to their ports to winkle them out.

The army together with Austrailians and New Zealanders and many more, have pushed the Italians back from Egypt to Lybia, we see pictures of hundreds of Italian army prisoners escourted by ten British soldiers, no fear of the prisoners trying to escape, they are very happy to be prisoners, Italians it seems love to sing but have very little stomach for war. The navy and the Army are doing to the Italians what the RAF did to the Germans, and it does us all a power of good, we will take all that they can sling at us, but it sure helps if our boys are slinging some back.

The new year has come and gone rather quietly, except for the Germans contribution but of course, you can hardly wish any one a Happy New Year, most people would think you were just a little mad I expect the wish of the people would just be an end to the war.

It's a nice frosty morning, so I fancy a trip over the Warren, I know it won't be as noisy as the last time I went, as the Germans now know better than to come by day, except for the occasional sneaky low level raid, when their fighter bombers will drop 1 bomb each and get back over the channel before the RAF can get them.

Tinker the collie has got the message and off we go, he likes it best when we get to the path behind the school, a lot of dogs pass that way, The dairy cows have been milked and are now busy eating the hay put out by the farmer, the skylarks are singing and the girls at the school are outside doing their P.T in their physical training gear. Further along the path I pass the anti-aircraft gun team they were busy last night, but today are not on the gun, they have developed an interest in gymnastic displays given by the girls at the school, I did get noticed by one member of the crew probably because he was somewhat older than the rest. Morning lad he said in a Yorkshire accent, "grand morning, sure is I said, and with a broad grin his eyes went down to his paper, I was pleased to see him relaxing.

Up the lane to the Warren, Tinkers off the lead, the searching every rabbit hole, me I have my usual place by the oak tree over looking the Warren, the gun, and the school. The ferns are brown now with a touch of frost on them, but in a month or two they will be green again, and the birds will be singing a little more than today.

Having sat there for a while I decided to move up the hill, and as I neared the top I saw a "special constable" patrolling the wire running along the railway line, he was looking all around him obviously keen to make sure nobody got near the railway. This aroused my curiosity, I just had to know why.

Putting Tinker back on the lead in case he ran past the copper, and waiting until he had gone by, I slowly made my way to the top and hiding behind a bush I looked down at the train on the line below, and what an exciting scene there was.

Sometime ago two massive under ground storage chambers had been built into the hill side, with hugh steel doors, and now I was looking at the reason for their construction,

A train was standing by these doors and hugh bombs and shells were being run on tracks into the under ground chambers. This obviously was not the first train, as the aera was filling up fast, What a scoop, I am probably the only one to see this, wait till I tell the lads.

It then dawned on me that I could tell nobody, as the poster said, "careless talk costs lives", if the Germans got to know about this rather large ammunition dump and were lucky enough to get a direct hit on it, then Ashford a mile away might be in serious trouble, so I kept it to myself and felt ten feet tall by doing so, but it sure was hard, the lads would have been green with envy, since then the vandles have been busy and those two sturdy doors are just an un-sightly mess, maybe they won't be needed again, we hope not.

In three weeks time I shall be fourteen years old, and must leave school, firstly because that is the leaving age, and secondly because lads like myself must replace the men who have gone into the services, Army, RAF, and Navy.

There are two jobs on offer, one in building, one in sign writing and painting, and I have taken the latter, if the governor accepts me, I am off to see him now.

It is a very small business only two other employees, the governor introduces me to them, I like Ern, he is twenty one years old and a very nice guy. The other one has a "bad foot", and is about thirty five, his name is Dan. I don't think I like him, he looks the type that should wear knee pads and must keep wiping something off the end of his nose. He keeps throwing snide remarks and the governor does a little smile, I smell a crawler, and that's something I just cannot stand, but Ern at the other end of the shop calls out, don't take any notice of him Huck, we will sort him out, and with a laugh all round my interview was over, and I was glad of that.

I will be in touch with the school the governor said, and if they are agreeable you can start the Monday following your leaving date. Just three weeks to my leaving date, suddenly school was great, the thought of leaving all my mates and burying myself in that small workshop made me want to stay on, Ray and Steve just could not understand it.

Well the day has arrived and I have to see the headmaster Bill Pumphrene, and at 11-30 sharp down I go. Outside his office sits the other boy he looks even less excited than me.

Hawn and Blake come in please and we quickly did as requested. On seeing Bill Pumphrene I remembered my previous visits, fortunatly this one should be less painful. Sit down he said, this was certainly different, last time it was hold out your hand, and after six whacks of the cane I was out the door. He was of course a no nonsense man and lost no time in making it plain that the school had made every effort to give us an education that would equips us life, on the other side of those doors. It is now up to you, and with that stood up and of course so did we. He had a few words with the other boy, then turned too me.

Well Hawn! you have come to know my office better than most boys, and you probably sensed my dis-pleasure, but I am pleased to say that you have worked well between visits, and I wish you and James here a prosperous future, and with a firm h and shake we were on our way, with very, very mixed feelings.
On that last day walking through those gates it was an awful feeling, the war was on, things were so uncertain, and what I would really have liked was to ask dad a few things, but of course he was away, and mum just would not have had the answer to my questions. So it was down too me and I wrote myself a few lines.
Huckleberry Hawn 14 years old.
All the world yet to unfold.
unfold it with courage, never afraid.
And with the help of your conscience.
Life's foundation is laid.
Seemed to cover every thing and I think now it did.

It's Monday morning and I have a whole week to myself before I start work.

I have imagined myself standing before a Judge in court and hearing him say, I sentence you to fifty one years of hard labour uou will retire at sixty five years, next case.
Of course it's not quite like that, I should become a good tradesman and be able to sell my skills to the best employer, the

man before the Judge will be in secure accomadation, and having reached the age of 14 I don't think I will be joining him.

I have been told by my employer to be, that I will need a few basic tools, and some protective clothing, I think I will make that my first job.

Next I must get down to the allotment, now that Ern has joined the RAF, I have taken it on. Most of the vegetables must be planted now, especially the early Potatoes, these will be quite a treat. They will be lifted when they are about the size of golf balls cooked and creamed with one of our butter rations and we shall enjoy them, anything like that makes rationing a little more bearable.

The next important thing on the allotment will be picking the Morrelo Cherries in a few weeks, these are for mum, they will become mum's cherry brandy with the help of the sugar which we all involuntaryly donate, but it gave us all a wonderful glow last christmas, so we would be silly to complain, apart from that she loves making it so it is well worth while.

Last but not least I shall go on my favourite walk to the Warren with Tinker. This rough piece of ground with its old Ash, Beech, Oak trees with the woodpeckers holes in their branches is where a boy can dream of all the things he intends to do, with so many years ahead, surly they are all possible? of course they are. Then reality reared its ugly head when I thought of the little business I was about to join, and the potential for me to reach great heights. I was more convinced of this after my first week's work.

I had made the tea, tended the "tortoise" stove, swept the shop and ran errands, one of which was disastrous. The Goveneor has asked me to take a cake tin back to his mother, I tucked the tin under my arm and off I went on my bike, on the way my front tyre burst and I came off, unfortunatly on top of the governors tin The tin was now quite useless and although it was really not my fault I felt my first week was not a very good start. The governor was quite nice about it, but did not offer anything towards the front tyre. Perhaps he thought 7 shillings and sixpence (37½ pence) he was going to pay me per week would cover it. He was a little tight, but only half as tight as his wife.

The other job of the week was standing on the bottom of the ladder while Ernest worked up above, this was also a little disastrous as the boredom gave me the chance to think of my lucky mates just sitting listening to Mr Battle, having been side tracked on to esperanto, or perhaps out on the games field. playing football. I was looking forward to leaving, but now I think I wish I was still there, I guess the grass is not always greener on the other side of the fence.

Victories are still in short supply, we still have our Battle of Britain victory, but our North African, Egypt to Libya victory over the Italians has been rather short. The Italians were no bother, but Hitler needs the Middle East, and so he is putting his army into Africa and with it's superiour equipment, forced a withdrawal of our troops, but cannot get them out of Tobruk try as he may.

Still the Royal Navy fills us with admiration they are sinking the Italian fleets as fast as they can find them, but that is not easy.

Our greatest threat is from the German U-boats, unseen ,they wait for our supply ships from around the world. We have lost a large percentage of our Merchant fleet, things look bad.

Many neutral ships, and ships from around the Empire have been sunk, but the fact that they do come with men and materials many thousands of miles is a boost to our faith in victory.

As Winston Churchill said " give us the tools and we will finish the job".

U- boats are not having it all their own way the Navy sinks them, and the RAF get them too. Hitler vows he will starve us into surrender, and with our present losses in shipping it sometimes crosses our minds, we can take all his bombs and bullets but we have to eat, but while there is concern in peoples faces, fear there is not.

It was a blow when France surrendered and the Vichy government set up the "unoccupied zone" doing Hitler's dirty work, it will be many years before the disgrace felt by many French people will be forgotten, but there are many French men and women still working in the Resistance Movement in contact with the allies, Britain, and the Free French in Britain, many will be shot by the Germans before the wars end, but they fight on.
VIVE-LA-FRANCE.

Bill and Herby are producing all the food they can on the farm, but the clamps of Potatoes and Sugar Beet are almost gone, and the stacks of wheat have been thrashed and the grain milled into flour, some of which has probably been used by my brother Les in the bakery, and it is a few months yet to harvest *1941.
Ships will be sunk, brave seamen will die, but the survivors will quickly sign on with another ship, they will go to sea again and this time will survive.

RULE BRITANNIA.

Well I have been at work a month now, and the routine is still the same, making tea, stoking the fire, pushing the barrow and standing on ladders, all of which adds up to absolute boredom. I am really looking forward to the day when I will be eighteen years old and my call up papers for the army, or the air force will drop on the mat, what has made me so depressed today is the news the governor has just given me, my mate Erne has not been at work for a couple of days, and I certainly missed him, neither Dan or the governor really speak my language, and so when the governor told me that Erne had Tuberculosis, I was near to tears Erne was only twenty one years old.

I think the governor had sensed that Erne and myself had sort of teamed up, and he had chosen a time when there was just he and I there to tell me, we don't know if he will be back Huck,, perhaps it wont be too long.

I knew enough about T B to know that at that time the survival rate was not good, in those days it was often a death sentence but I had to hope he would be back.

Listening to Dan crawling around the governor made me sick, when the governor was around they would discuss Beethoven, Mozart, or Wagner's music, but when the governor was out Dan would be whistling the latest pop music. I though this had the smell of a first rate crawler, and I knew my mate Erne could never be a two faced crawler, we both spoke the same language.

I am glad it is Saturday, perhaps Monday things may look better. I have to work this morning, but this afternoon I think I will go to the allotment, and put a few seeds in, when I am gardening I can be completely relaxed, and right now that sounds good.

Oh to be in England now that April's here [A well known line, but oh so true just now.

With the world in such a mess, London and our big cities still being heavily bombed at night, producing scenes of absolute devastation, thousands of people dead, and injured, it seems like another world, to see friut orchards in full blossom, hedge rows turning green again, gardens a mass of flower, I think we all feel a little guilty enjoying such a beautiful sight.

We are still aware of the German's by night when the sirens sound, and the anti-aircraft guns let out their ear shattering noise, when we lay in our beds hoping they don't jetison their bombs over Ashford. That was the way it was, we know somebody has got to cop it, but I hope it is not me.

Dad is home today with his week-end pass, and it's always good to see him. He is just telling us of a bit of excitment on the camp.

Last week two F W 190 German planes requested permission to land, and after massive precautions it was granted, so now we have two of their latest planes, for our designers and armament experts to go over most carefully for any information that will help the RAF.

The second bit of news was not so exciting as it concerned Dads life in the RAF, Dad has still not fully recovered from his accident in France, and at his last medical examination it was decided that he would have to return to civilian life and leave the RAF.

I think he has enjoyed his life in the RAF, his work in processing the photos taken on and after the bombing raids across the channel, were of great interest too him, He will I am sure miss the camp life, as he was the kind of guy that would get on with anyone, what he told us of camp life, seemed to have plenty of laughs. We all said that's great news Dad, but it was obvioously not good news for Dad.

Mum sensed this and made a bit of a fuss of him, saying it would be great to have him home, that made him grin and we all settled back to listen to the radio.

It will take a bit of getting used to as mum has been the boss and we boys have had it quite easy, Dad will want his chair back again, he has to have the first cup of tea out of the pot as he likes it very strong, and our music is sure to be too loud but all of that is fine by us.

We really will be glad to have him back, one good thing will be that he can sit in the cupboard when the siren sounds and we can stay in bed without feeling guilty.

I think Dad will miss being "part of it" he will just be a very keen radio listner of the news, and read the headlines in the newspaper. He will hear on the radio how the RAF are flying more and more trips across the channel, especially the invasion craft, and how the RAF is hitting Germany itself, Berlin, Bremen and Hamburg etc.

It is great to hear the announcer say a large force of aircraft from bomber command attacked these cities and others, and to know that things were begining to change gave us all a boost. However after the announcement we always knew there would be one more sentence. A number of our aircraft failed too return.

It was a a sobering thought that the success of these raids was at thr expense of the gallant men who made up the air crews.

Our airmen were in a very different situation than the Germans. Berlin was a long way from our airfields, but London was not far from the captured French airfields. One day before the war ends they will lose these French airfields, and they will see in the sky above them a thousand bombers on thier way to Germany most of them carrying 1000 pound bombs. The devastation they have caused in Britain will be repaid, it will be ten fold, and very many German people will die, but one must hope that this really will be "The War to end Wars".

It is good to hear we are attacking a little more instead of just defending, and we are now having greater success against the German's who are still bombing our cities.

Last month 80 German aircraft were shot down by the RAF night fighters, and anti-aircraft fire. The German's had too change from daylight to night bombing because of their losses, perhaps soon they will decide night bombing is also too expensive.

Not such good news from North Africa, we are still having to withdraw from Libya after such a splendid advance against the Italians. The German equipment is proving to be more of a problem than the Italians equipment.

The Libyian port of Tobruk is however still held by us, try as the German's may they cannot get the Australians and the Brits out of their holes. They have been called The Desert Rats" and they are proud to accept the title. Field Marshal Rommel the German general must be very keen to winkle them out. The Desert Rats are supplied by sea, the Royal Navy is still very much in control in the Mediterranean, The Italian lake as they like too call it, has changed hands.

Last month Hitler's deputy Hess flew into Scotland hoping to do a deal with Britain, but Churchill would have none of that, and promptly locked him up. Today I think the reason for the trip by Rudolph Hess is a little more apparent.

Hitler has invaded Russia, probably the greatest mistake of the war, he obviously thinks he can succeed where Napoleon failed. I think had he been able to do a deal with us, he might have won his Russian war, but after winning he would quickly have turned on us, not a man to trust.

The Russians like ourselves ,were very poorly equiped but they will soon change that, they have however one very important weapon THE RUSSIAN WINTER.

The Russian winter will kill thousands of German soldiers, and Hitler will be indirectly responsible for some. He has a military machine the like of which has never been seen before, but with no military experience himself he still persists in over ruling his comanders in the field, with some disastrous results.

Ironically it was the Russians who had the last word regarding Hess, they insisted he spend the rest of his life in prison, but then this was to some degree under standable for they had probably suffered more than most other countries.

The summer has been quite good on the farms, the harvest is in full swing. Bill has been working dawn to dusk, and that is where he is now. Bill and Nelson are both cutting, others will be stacking the sheafs into groups for transporting to the farm. Where in large stacks it will remain until being thrashed, and the grain milled into flour for our very important bread.

It is getting late and the light is not too good and as Nelson came along side Bill he shouted had enough Bill?, I most certainly have said Bill, or words to that effect.

Right lets call it a day and after parking their machine, Bill put his bike in the truck and it was away home, but first a quick pint in the pub. Evening Tom, evening Bill how goes it? very dry Tom so I'll have two pints of the best you have got. Bill took the two pints and made his way to the table where Nelson was sitting, over their pint they would discuss tomorrows work.

Harvesting must be completed as soon as possible, every grain grown would save valuable shipping space, but tonight they had a visit from one of three soldiers at the bar.

The soldier sauntered over to Bill's table rather unsteady on his feet, and looked Bill straight in the eyes, then with a very loud voice he said "When are you going to join the army"? Now Bill has been asked this question many times, and his usual reply was, when they have killed you mate I'll go, and that most times killed the conversation. Tonight however something snapped, Bill stood up and with one almighty punch sent the soldier flying, and now he lay rather still on the floor. You could almost hear a pin drop in the bar, most of those in the pub knew Bill, and would never have expected this, it was completly out of place with Bill, you could say what you liked to him, and all you would get would be a wise-crack and a laugh. The second soldier came over to help the first soldier up, bit over the top was'nt it he said. Bill just glared at him and it was obvious that no meaning full conversation was going to be forth coming, so the soldiers made their way too a table. The soldier just sat with his head in his hands with his elbows on the table.

Bill felt some what embarrased and when he met Nelson's eyes, Nelson said blimey Bill you did'nt half hit him, yes said Bill and I am very sorry, but he asked the wrong question at the wrong time. I have been asked that question fifty times, and he got all what the other forty nine should have got, and with that he said lets go Nelson.

No not yet Nelson said I have hardly touched my drink, O K said Bill, and with that he stood up and said sorry about that everyone, I guess I just snapped, sorry, and sat down, conversation in the bar began again. The third soldier stayed at the bar perhaps he felt discretion was the better part of valour, as he looked around he would have seen some rather beefy farmers and farm workers who would not have taken kindly to a rumpus in the middle of their hard earned pint.

They all knew Bill and Nelson and it was obvious who would come off worse but all three soldiers were decent guys, they were not looking for trouble, and from a local point of view the lads in Khaki, Navy Blue, or Air Force Blue were all very welcome in their pub.

Bill picks up the glasses, my turn Bill said Nelson, next time said Bill, I want a word with Tom, O K said Nelson it being obvious what the word would be about.

Over at the bar Bills says in a rather quiet voice, two more pints please Tom, and when Tom brought the beer Bill said, sorry Tom but I have been asked that question so many times, that with a long day cutting corn it was just the straw that broke the camels back, not your fault Bill, or his, and Tom turned to the third soldier, tell Bill what you've just told me Syd.

Syd went on to explain why it had probably all happened. Jim the soldier Bill hit had just lost his whole family, his house his wife and three boys in an air raid on London, his only home now was with his mother, and she was worried sick.

Bill was close to tears, damn sodden Germans, I wish I had known Syd, not your fault Bill said Syd, Jim is a damn nice guy, and if you met him tomorrow he would just grin and say how stupid he had been, but I don't suppose you will Bill as our anti-air craft unit is being moved closer to London, we pull out tomorrow that is really why we are here tonight having a last drink here.

Well al the best Syd, and to Jim and Alex, and with a shake of hands Bill felt a little better. Nelson and Bill finished their beer and began to make their way to the door, good night every one.

On their way out they passed Jim and the second soldier. Bill stopped put his hand out and said sorry Jim, Syd has just told me about your family, I really am sorry, I wish I had known. Jim shook Bill's hand and said no, my fault Bill, it was a stupid thing to say, well said Bill if you get the chance, kill a few for me, sure will Bill, bye, and all the best.

Two strangers had met, one insulted the other, and he had landed a very hard blow to the chin of this man who had issued the insult, now just over an hour later they were parting as friends, never to meet again, like ships that pass in the night, another aspect of war.

Bill closed the door, and Tom the barman turned to Syd and said, Bill's the salt of the earth, he works from dawn to dusk and never a moan, all you get from Bill is a wise crack and a laugh what happened here tonight is so unlike Bill, that question I suppose came on top of a long day, and he had had it many times. I know Jim and Bill will not meet again but I would be grateful Syd if you would tell Jim what I have said, I will be said, now we had better be getting back to camp. Jim and Alex rose from their table, and the soldiers who the locals had come to know quite well called "Bye everyone" and the three comrades in arms drifted off into the night, leaving the locals wondering how these young soldiers would fare in the years ahead.

Bill and Herbert will not be called up, but brother Les is just about to go.. He has had his call up papers and his medical examination, and h as been passed A-1 and is fit for service.

He has been told to report to the RAF base where he will do his training, he is a big lad over six feet tall, obviously able to give a good account of himself, but mum still wants to help pack his bag. I think she would like to go to the station with him but she knows better than to suggest it.

Cecil Horn

Well bye everyone and with a big hug for Mum, and a firm shake of Dad's hand he is off. She watches him go and as he turns the corner, he waves his hand and is gone. Mum looks a bit watery eyed but she knows there is nothing she can do, if a man does not report to the military base as directed, the military police will be sent to escort him to that camp, Mum has got her husband back from the RAF, but they now have two of her son's, excluding Bill and Herby, Will they get Huck and Reg and Derek and will they all come back? it is hard for a mother to feel patriotic when she sees her sons being taken from her.

England expects every man to do his duty, it is still the same as it was in Admiral Nelson's day. I think she is glad she has two two of her son's in a reserved occupation producing food but as Bill has found it is not easy at times to live with. Bill does not mind the taunts about not going into the services, not having joined up because he knows the governmrnt sees him as far more valuable where he is, what Bill hates is the thought that these people who make their sarcastic remarks, may be thinking that he is a conscientious objector, a person who refuses to fight on religious grounds. He would fight with the best of men and hide behind no man, as the soldier found when he asked that question, when are you going to join the army? Bill would defend himself without hesitation, not the action of a "conchie"

Mum is looking somewhat subdued, rather deep in thought, many things would be going through her mind, she might possibly think of Peter, the brother of Harry, a friend of Les.

Peter decided he could not wait until he was eighteen (call up age) and so he volunteered, he was just passed his seventeen years, there would be no check on his age all men were badly needed, Mum's Les went off at eighteen, but Peter never reached his eightenth birthday, he was "killed in action" as the war office would say. His mother was in a very sad way, so very upset, she had just two boy's, and now one was dead, just a boy.

Today Mum knowing Peter's Mum so well might say to herself there but for the grace of God go I, but with seven son's the odds shorten and the fear grows. Dad does his best too re-assure her. he will be alright Violet, he has all his training to do yet, and the war might be over by then, not a very good way to make her feel better though, for she reads the papers, and listens to the radio and she knows the war is not going too well for us right now. She would of course hear the news reader say, last night aircraft of bomber command attacked targets in the Ruhr, Bremen and Cologne, seven of our aircraft are missing. Her mathematics are quite good and she would soon translate seven aircraft into aircrew killed in action.

In North Africa all the territory taken from the Italians has been re-taken by Field Marshal Rommel and his Afrika Corp, except Tobruk that is, and there The Desert Rats refuse to budge, even Rommel and all his equipment cannot move them.

The air raids are getting less frequent, Hitler has other need for his aircraft, The Russian War.

Hitler has stood on the other side of the channel, and through his telescope looked at the island in the sea, which after all his bombing and burning, still seemed green. I don't suppose he would have run my favourite lines through his mind though.

My lines would be, as that great poet wrote them.

This sceptred Isle set in silver sea,
This Island kept by nature for herself.
This other Eden, This England.

Hitler's words would be a little different, He would stand there thumping the bonnet of his bullet proof Merc, ranting and raving. These little Englander's they are short of food, their supplies lie at the bottom of the sea, their cities are burnt, and destroyed, the greatest war machine of all times faces them twenty one miles away across the channel, do they still think they can win?

His generals would be a little reluctant to answer his question, Hitler did not receive criticism well and they were of the opinion that he had waited too long, and that the Invasion of England was a year overdue, but perhaps the RAF had something to do with that, the best laid plans go wrong. Anyway Hitler had a much bigger problem, the Russian Bear was gnawing at his newly made frontier in Poland.

Thousands of Russian troops were assembling and so he would finish Russia off then come back for England, or so he thought. He must have thought his invincible war machine would slice through the Russian peasants like a knife through butter, so he tore up his peace treaty with Russia, and made a gigantic miscalculation the Russians fought with all they had got.

Hitler almost reached Moscow but not quite, and it was here that the Russians winter turned that great war machine around and Russian troops began to follow it to the German border, the begining of the end. It will be a couple of years before the last German is killed on Russian soil, but the limit of the murderous advance has been reached. Another thirty miles and the German's would have been in Moscow, but the Russians gave their all and held on and now the Germans involved in trying to take Moscow will have a terrible experience.

They began the attack on Russia in June, and now in December they are in retreat, the invinceable are heading back to Germany, followed by the Russian army, that will repay them in full for all the Russian people they have killed in their bloody advance. They will find little shelter from the Russian winter. As far as the eye can see snow with a temperature 30-40 below freezing, they will freeze too death in their trenches, and be crushed by Russian tanks, and Hitler will continue to demand no retreat.

Well here in my little world things have not changed much, Ray and Steve have now reached 14 years of age, and must like me leave school to start work. Ray is in a factory making parts for the equipment used on the farms around here, plus some for the war department.

Steve is in the local Iron Foundery which before the war made such things as drain covers, but now is also involved in ministry work. Me, well the governor has decided that I can now wield my paint brush on larger vehicles of a slightly higher standard.

We have moved from the rather small premises in Norward Street, too larger buildings in Worger's Alley, but unfortunately my mate Erne will not be with us. He took me under his wing when I first joined the firm, but had to go into hospital with tuberculosis, and now he has died at 21 years old, at 14 years old it has hit me pretty hard, when the governor told me I was close to tears. I liked Erne a lotand too die at 21 years seemed hardly possible, even amongst the distruction of war, still one quickly accepts death as inevitable, just another statistic, we just try to survive, and not become one of them.

My first job in the new premises was a horse drawn vehicle belonging to the local bakery where brother Les worked before going into the RAF. If was a bit rough, but now it looks great, the upper part is maroon red, the lower part is sunshine yellow, including the wooden wheels, and shafts which will take the horse A twin black line runs around the outer part of the wheels, and a line down each spoke, also a twin black line along the shafts. The horse is now between the shafts, he is light brown with a golden mane, the whole picture looks marvellous, I think my interest in painting has improved.

The bakery and others are still using horse drawn transport where possible as fuel is not that plentiful, and vehicle mechanics are also in short supply.

I think colour has given me a greater interest in my job. The horse drawn vehicle looked great, and not far away in Chart Road E.C. ran a sand and ballast company, his vehicles were Maroon red with pure gold leaf lettering, his vehicles were motor engined lorries, these two company's were typical of a very colourful period, but pre war stocks of good quality paint were coming to an end, paint would soon be made from fish oil, a very different material.

As I write a very plesent memory comes to mind, the bells across the green have begun their weekly practice, and I am reminded of Mum's favourite record "BELL'S ACROSS THE MEADOW" The picture on the sleeve was of a church just across a meadow of butter cups, bathed in the evening sunlight. The bells in this church would be gently ringing to call the people to evensong, this absolutely relaxing picture fired Mum's imagination I think. It was the usual Sunday evening after another long day, and that record seemed a must, she would wind up the gramaphone, place the record o, close the lid and settle back in her easy chair, but it was very likely that before the end of the record she would have "drifted off", perhaps across the green, through the evening sunshine and through those heavy church doors where it was absolute peace. The war had not yet invaded the church.
One of us would quietly remove the record and place it back in it's sleeve, probably until next Sunday, but none of us ever said "Oh no" not that again, she deserved every relaxing minute.

Church bells of course cannot be rung unless the German's are invading the country, and then it would not be as Mum would like it, but rung in such a way as to make sure every one would hear them and know of their imminent danger.

Those lines "SEEK YE NOT FOR WHOME THE BELL TOLLS, IT TOLLS FOR THEE" would mean just that. Thousands would die, Ashford was to be held at all costs, those who did not leave immediately would have to remain in town. German paratroopers would have been droped in great numbers, and our troops not long back from Dunkirk would be called on again, the outcome of such a battle would be hard to predict.

Fortunately the situation never arose, Hitler waited too long, he over ruled his generals, and with no military knowledge at all he halted the invasion by the best equiped army for years, it was postponed indefitely. Historians believe Hitler was still hoping to do a deal with Churchill, and was reluctant to commence the invasion, but Churchill would only accept the absolute defeat Of Germany, no deals.

The government have decided that all teenagers should join a youth organisation, and so I have joined the ATC (air cadets) Steve and Ray have joined the sea cadets, we were not what you might call patriotic, but England expects and all that so we did what Admiral Nelson would have expected.

The ATC meets on two evenings a week, and I think the sea cadets about the same, so it is not a bad thing, boys need to be occupied. The first part of our ATC evening is taken up with parade ground marching, and saluting, it is impressed on us that if we are in uniform we must a salute all officers, this did not come easily. Next it was tea and cakes with the nice lady across the road, she is quite young with a good sense of humour. Back to work now and it is aircraft recognition, we need to reconize allied and enemy aircraft by their shape and know their capability, and we have to learn morse code so that we can send and receive messages as fast as possible. Well that was some of the work, but we also had a games room with a full sized Billiard table, I think this rather influenced my regular attendance.

I now have my uniform it is just like the RAF, but some what smaller, especially as I am a little on the short side.

Dad thought it would make a nice photo and so when "properly dressed" I was positioned on the seat with little sister Rita Dad thought with Rita it would make more of a family picture. When I look back at that photo today I have to smile I see this boy in what appears to be a military uniform, and it reminds me of a film I saw some time ago called "They Gave Him A Gun". it was about the 14-18 war, the boy in the film hardly knew one end of a gun from the other, but he had a gun and felt ten feet tall, and did not connect the gun with the inevitable, his death.

I have wondered what Mum thought seeing this angelic young boy in uniform, might she have said to herself, not content with taking my son's at eighteen, they now want them at fifteen. What a pity they were not around when they wanted their nappy changed.

We have been at war for over two years now, and victory seems a long way off. We are very pleased to hear that the army in North Africa have re-taken all the land lost to the Germans thus relieving Tobruk, we were all aware what those lads have been through, not so good for the Navy, we have lost a number of ships including the aircraft carrier Ark Royal.

The Germans are gaining ground in some parts of Russia but else where they are in retreat, the Russians now have better equipment, and well clothed soldiers.

The American's AND OURSELVES ARE SENDING ALL WE CAN, BUT TO get it there presents an extremly hazardous situation for our Royal Navy, and our Merchant Navy, as the extreme cold itself is a killer. The sea spray and the freezing rain and snow would freeze on the ship and have too be removed or it could make the ship unstable.

U boats would be waiting for our ships and inevitability torpedo would hit, and the men would have to get into the life boats quickly, some would have to jump into the sea, but life expectancy for these unfortunate men in the freezing water could be just a few minutes.

Now we have another problem.
The date is is Decenber 7th 1941 and the Japanese have bombed the American fleet in Pearl Harbour, sinking some of the best ships in the American Navy and killing many men.

The Japanese now have a tiger by the tail, sooner or later their grip will be loosend, and as they get go, it will turn and devour them. To make war on America and the British Empire of that time seemed nothing short of lunacy, for which they will pay heavily. Like Germany the Japs had built up a first rate army Navy and Air Force, they probably saw our far east bases as easy conquests, and saw the Americans as rather pre-occupied with the good life in the Philippines, but the sleeping giants are now well and truly awake.

The Japanese have now done what Churchill has been trying to achieve for some time, they have brought that power house into the war with us, we no longer stand alone.

Churchill has gone to America and has addressed the American Senate, he has been received with considerable enthusiasm, we now present a united front.

It is christmas again and while in America, Churchill will be asking for christmas presents in the form of guns, tanks, ships, aircraft etc. give us the tools and we will finish the job he said every time he spoke he put new life into us.

Yes it is the third christmas, and with each one the feast of Stephen becomes a little less of a feast. Christmas in terms of booze and binge is not so important, the real christmas story is much more important, it was quite noticeable at the church on christmas eve when it was standing room only. I guess that we would all pray for the end of the war, but each one of them would have someone some where in danger, who would be at risk in the coming months, and in church on christmas eve would feel a little better, knowing someone was watching over them, and a little less fearful of what lay ahead.

It was noticeable last week when there was an account of a ship sunk in the Atlantic, and the men took to the life boats that one of those life boats had been adrift for many days, the food, water and hope had now all gone, so they prayed, that night it rained, they could live without food but not without water. I am sure parents, wives, girl friends and children had prayed many times since that ship went down.

It is now mid January and very cold. The frost is white on the ground and the farm is getting ready for the days work. Bill and his work mates are about to put the wheat harvested last autumn through the thrashing machine, this will soon warm the men, but at the moment there are a few remarks about freezing the extremities from a brass Monkey.

The thrashing machine was a large belt driven monster which would brought along side the stack of wheat, which was then fed into it seperating the grain from the straw.

It would be almost dark when Bill and Herby came home looking more like miners than farm workers, the work was very dusty and it seemed to stick too them. It was of course no problem for them to wash and clean up, it was however a little harder for Mum. The floor of the bedroom next morning would be covered with straw and chaff which had got into the clothing of Bill and Herby while thrashing and there was no vacum cleaner, it was just dust pan and brush, fortunatly they both shared the same room. Tomorrow they have another messy job, they have to open the potato clamp, and take out the required amount of potatoes and re-seal it. The clamp method was the usual way of storing things like potatoes, sugar beet, wortzels etc., it would be a base of straw, then the potatoes and about a couple of feet of earth over the whole aera. Mum is again on the wrong end of the operation as it can only be done when the temperature is above freezing, this of course means that the hard ground is now muddy and so more work for Mum, still at least they come home every evening, unlike Les and Ern, so I think she would rather have it this way.

We don't see so much of Ern now as he is married and obviously spends his 7 days leave with his wife Winnie.

For a young lady in time of war to marry a man in the services needed a great deal of thought.

The war showed no sign of ending, and now the war in the far East meant that a man could be fighting in any one of a dozen countries, but she would marry him for it was so much of a comfort to know that they were one, and if he did not come back he would still be hers.

It was of course a terrible thing to see, every street had it's war widows, just down the road from us is a young woman who has just joined the ranks of these tragic young women, fortunatly she lives with her man's mother who will help look after the children whose tears will be slow to stop, Mum's tears of course will be shed when she is alone and the children asleep. War has brought great tragedy to many people it has also made many very rich, Ministry work could be a nice little earner.

In a small way my govenor has decided to help his self to some of this, and so I am now spray painting air ministry lorries after they have been over hauled, we then brush green patches over them for camouflage, this was supposed to make them less visible from the air. Factory roofs were done in the same way but a good man could read an ariel photograph quite easily, so it was not a great deal of good, but I think he had an eye to the future as men involved in ministry work could sometimes be granted "reserved occupation status", this meant an employer kept his men and they did not therefore go into the services.

Skilled men were very hard to find and to those employers a man lost could be a problem, Bill and Herby would be very hard to replace, and the government knows they are of much more value to the war effort where they are.

Mum of course is very pleased they are reserved, but they sure make a lot of work for her, especially the washing, she would think she was in heaven if she had a washing machine of today, but lighting the copper, boiling the clothes scrubbing them with a bar of soap, putting them through the mangle out in the yard on a January morning, and finally hanging them on the line meant one hell of a day. Then of course there was the ironing, you did not push a plug in the wall and switch on, she had this cast iron flat iron which was place don the gas ring to get hot, the trick of course was knowing at what point it would burn the shirts etc. it if was too hot.

Dad did not get his clothes dirty but he had another problem for Mum, he would insist on very stiff starched shirt collars, detached, and stiff as boards. Mum would say, she hated them, but he just did not feel properly dressed without them.

He was one of those men who did very little in the kitchen. In those days I suppose very few did. He most times after meals would head for his dark room and do a few photography jobs.

One of my less happy memories was that Dad never found time to take us out, or make us a soap box on wheels, make us a rabbit hutch etc, but I guess with eight children a man could become financially and physically drained.

I think when he went to the dark room to work it was not just work, it was the one place where he could get peace and quiet. He pulled the curtain to keep any daylight out, as this would ruin his films, and then light up his cigarette, fill the air with smoke and know there would be no complaints from the family, this was his castle. While enjoying his fag you might hear him quietly singing one of his songs from the 14-18 great war. when he was in France in 1917 we never heard much of it just "Madamoiselle from Armantiers parley vous" and a repeat of that line.

He was of course much younger then and quite a good looker I wonder if he ?? No I don't think so, he was really quite a quiet chap. Later in the evening when the washing up etc, was all done he would come indoors and on his way to his easy chair take some coal from the scuttle and place it on the fire, he seldom filled the scuttle but he did'nt mind emptying it. He now felt warm and comfortable in his easy chair beside the fire, but this sometimes meant trouble, as Mum who was quite well covered and quickly over heated, this in turn soon meant the "atmosphere was also a little over heated.

We are now in our third year of war, and it is still not going too well, there is not much to cheer about, and the end seems a long way off. Since the Japanese entered the war on December 7th they have advanced rapidly, Hong Kong fell on December 25th and by February 13th they had taken Singapore, and at sea they distroyed two of our best Battle ships, by bombing, not by the Jap Navy.

We had a good navy, but our air cover left a bit to be desired I think our far away our posts had not been at all ready for war. Japan would have been well aware of the situation. They were already at war with China, and from there they had an easy ride, taking Malaya, Borneo, Sumatra and they are now in New Guinea, very close to Australia, and much of the Australian army is fighting around the world. All this in three months, has done very little for our morale.

That area is very much in our minds at the moment as brother Ern has been sent to India, and the Japs in Burma are not that far from the Indian Frontier. Probably Mum's knowledge of geography would be a little rusty and she would not be aware that India was joined to Burma, but I am sure Ern's wife Win would know.

It is not likely that Ern would see any Japs except in photos taken by our aircraft over the actual fighting in Burma. He has a nice little number on an RAF Station near New Delhi, his job was to process these photos so that our position in Burma could be assessed, and action taken.

Brother Les is still in England, but probably not for much longer many men are being sent to North Africa, where the German General Rommel has retaken the land including Tobruk which we took from the Germans, We do have a little to cheer about, with our allies we can now mount 1000 bomber raids on German cities, we have waited a long time, we had to stand and take all that those murderous swine could rain down upon us, now we have the means to return it, and how we will,

Our bombers are now much bigger than the Germans of 1940, they carry far greater bomb loads ,German cities will now be reduced to rubble, German people will be torn apart, buried alive burned alive, and we will be glad. Such is the hatred that now lies within us. Hitler has stirred up a hornets nest, and and they will be coming his way. He and all those who followed him will reap the harvest of that which they have sown, and those who did not follow him but who just looked the other way will not be immune.

This happy breed of men as Noel Coward described us have been changed for ever, and for this we will never be glad.

At that time we could never have imagined that one day Germany and Britain would belong to the same club. socially and militarilly with war unthinkable and be glad. The whole world would be learning English. and perhaps when the world speaks English then man might understand his fellow man a little more.

It is a very quiet Hawn household today. We have a big problem Mum is upstairs in bed and the doctor has come too see her. There is a feeling of great uncertainty as to how this all male family (we have our sister Rita) is going to survive. Mum our powerhouse has for the moment ceased to function, and we don't know yet for how long. We know that what ever the doctor says it will not be something trivial, as Mum would not give in easily in the back of her mind would be the cost of calling the doctor out, any extra costs for the family were difinitly to be avoided.

The doctor has now told us what we were dreading ,she must remain in bed for a few days, he probably told Dad what her problem is, but he has not told us. If it is a "female" problem then he never will, boys of that time were told very little about the workings of the female body and would not dream of asking, they would know that they would not get a proper answer.

I guess only a young man's curiosity insured the human race did not die out, anyway what ever it was we were in for a difficult period. Usually any other female takes over in an emergency, but Rita is only nine years old, and so it is we who must look after her. Dad gives a good impression of a sailor up the creek without a paddle, he outlines what we are going to have to do, but we all know that he will probably have some photography that needs his urgent attention over in the dark room.

Back in the 1940s the male spent very little time in the kitchen and of course did very little cooking, Mum would never ask for help and the males were a little backward in voluntering. Meals could be a little disastertrous as Dad has decreed that whoever is at home, and not at work will be cook of the day.

We could yet be saved as brother Les is home on a weeks leave from the RAF. He was when he joined up placed with the RAF regiment, a unit specially formed to guard the airfields, but has since transferred to the catering department.

Just because he had some knowledge of cooking did not mean we were going to suggest that he spent his leave cooking for the family, but none of us tried to talk him out of it when he volunteered, he did however remind us that he had only been with catering for three weeks.

We have all been up to see Mum and assured her that we will be O.K, just rest and get better, she was obviously pleased to hear that.

Well we have had three days cooking by Les, and we have survived I have not heard anyone say "my compliments to the chef" but no one would dare to complain as Les has a slightly shorter fuse than the rest of us, a new cook would soon have to be found not to mention the possible damage to the one who complained.

Today it is Sausage and Mash and I have the job of taking it up to Mum, I noticed as it was placed on the plate the sausage was burnt on one side, this was carefully put burnt side down hoping Mum would not immediately see it. I am also hoping Mum's sense of smell is not too good at the moment, and the smell of burnt spuds does not reach her before me.

Mum was looking much better and obviously her sense of smell was not affected by her illnesses as she politly asked had the potatoes burnt? then with a devilish grin she gently rolled the sausage over to reveal the burnt side, perhaps they always burn on one side.

Anyway she had a chuckle and that was good to see. I could not help wondering if when she was alone she had a little chuckle at our predicament, this family of almost all males had really been thrown into the deep end, and were desperatly trying to swim. The doctor is coming this afternoon and we are all hoping that Mum will soon take over again..

The doctor has just come down and is having a few words with Dad, it was however not good news, well it was in one way, Mum was doing fine, the bad news was Mum would not be doing the cooking until the weekend, and it was only Wednesday. Dad looked rather glum, and of course remembered some prints in the developer in the dark room, this left the rest of us debating as to what we should do now. I was hoping that nobody would complain about the cooking if Les did'nt do it one of us would have to.

Well we have survived, and today is Saturday. Dad has taken Mum's breakfast up and we are all waiting to see what Mum will do, on his return to the living room I immediatly asked when Mum would be coming down? she did'nt say son, and I did not ask

her he said, it seemed as if she was making us wait, we were going to understand just how much we had taken her for granted.
I have volunteered to take Mum's dinner up to her, perhaps Dad had not said the right things, maybe she might yet soften up ,no luck. I am sorry to say she still has not yet said when she will be down.

Bill and Herby are at work, it is harvesting time again, Ern of course is in India, and the rest of a of us are just hanging around, can't seem to concentrate on anything, but suddenly we are a picture of alertness, our ears are tuned to the ceiling there is movement up above in Mum's room, the floor boards are doing a little creak our troubles are over, she is coming down the door opens and there she is, a sight for sore eyes, we all go to her ask her how she is? and put her in her favourite chair.

She smiles and say's she is much better, she thanks us all for the way we have kept things going and was very glad to be well again. What happened next took us completely by surprise, you could have heard a pin drop.
Thank you again she said, but I now have a few words to say to you all. She opened up with all guns blazing, she read us the riot act, gently but firmly she told us just how we had treated her, how we all did very little about the house, how we never did anything without first being asked, even just to fill the coat scuttle she would have to ask. I should not have to ask you. The doctor says I must rest a little more, can you tell me how I can do that? again there was complete silence, we all felt we had let her down badly, then with a chorus of sorry Mum we just did'nt think, we all stood up and moved closer too her assuring her that in future she would not have to ask. She was close to tears, she did not like having to hit us that hard, but she knew it was the only way. We would never have given her situation a thought, a willing horse can always work, and you never miss the water until the well runs dry, it nearly did.

Bill and Herby have just come home, they finish a little earlier on Saturday, but they will be working daylight till dark tomorrow, the harvest must be got in soon as possible. They come into the room, Hello Mum feeling better? sure glad to see you, you are looking great, there were smiles all round, and Mum said she was feeling much better. Then it all went quiet, so quiet that Bill said have we missed something? by the look in Bill and Herby's faces they sensed something was wrong. The silence lasted only a few seconds, but it seemed much longer, so I felt something should be said.

What you missed Bill, was a few words from Mum, she is very glad she is better, but the doctor has told her she must rest more and she cannot do that unless she gets a lot more help from us. We have all said we will give her all the help we can, of course we will said Bill, but Mum was probably thinking about all the straw on the bedroom floor, still it was now smiles all round, and to set a good example Dad is making the tea.

The harvest is still most important, every ton of grain produced on the farm by Bill and Herby is a space in a ship for a ton of war materials, they don't wear a uniform but they are very important guys.
The convoys of ships are getting through the U-boat packs bringing tanks guns and ammunition, men and much more, before long this Island will be sinking under the weight of an army with the superiority that Hitler had in 1940 but this time it will be ours and when this time comes we will go back to France. I think in this fourth year of war we are beginning to loose that "backs to wall" feeling, there are more grins on faces, more jokes about Adolph, people are happy to talk about the war, it is a long way from over but we can see a way through now. All around the world the tide is turning.

In North Africa The Desert Rats are on the move they are advancing and have made their last retreat. The move towards Rommel's Africa corp was heralded by the greatest artillary fire ever seen, the sky was lit up by continuous flashes from the guns as the shells fire overhead as our tanks and troops move forward. The shells would be falling in a few miles away and I wondered what it would be like a shell bursting every minute fragments tearing into bodies, explosions punctured by screams, and our troops coming upon this scene of devasation and having to kill any survivors, but it was kill or be killed, and there is precious little pity left for any German now.

Rommels Africa Corps is now in full retreat, many prisoners are being taken, it looks like the begining of the end for the Germans in North Africa. To be fair to Field Marshall Rommel he was not there at the time, he was in Germany, but on his return he could not stop the rot, the retreat was unstopable. Again to be fair to Rommel he was looked upon as a good soldier, even his enemy spoke well of him. He was a first rate tactician and fought fairly. I feel the world had a measure of sympathy for him when Hitler forced him to to commit suicide after a bomb plot on Hitler's life.

In this forth year of war, those Dessert Rats have helped to broaden our smiles it's a marvellous feeling, no more on the defensive we are moving forward, getting the upper hand, slowly but surely we are winning!.

Russia is well aware of the build up of materials in Britain and would like us to invade France, by doing so make Hitler fight on two fronts, they are taking a severe bashing but we are not yet ready, we can only send them war material to help them in their fight. The Russian summer has allowed the Germans to take back much of the land they lost to the Russians last winter, but the first snow is on the hills and the Germans know what that means. They have Leningrad and Stalingrad in a desperate situation but they know that if they do not capture these and other Russian cities within days the situation will be reversed and the Russian winter together with the Russian soldier will crush them.

They have failed to do this and are now in full retreat. It is an awful feeling when I think of fighting a greatly improved Russian army as a German soldier knee deep in snow in a temperature 30 degrees below freezing, my fingers freezing to my gun and my clothing the very much worse for wear, terrifying! I have no pity for them, but cannot help putting myself in their position and just being glad it's not me.

As they retreat the Russians will take a terrible revenge on them, every Russian death military or civilian will be avenged, again horrific deaths will take place, but this Russian revenge will be every bit as sweet to us in Britain, it is an awful thought that hate breeds hate in ever increasing amounts. We in Britain have not experienced these terrible acts of war face to face, but we feel most strongly for those that have, and we say "there for the grace of god go we" for had Hitler attached Britain instead of Russia it would have produced a quite different end of the war! of that I am convinced.

To add to our changed view of the war the Japs have taken a hell of a bashing at the hands of the Americans and Australians. Two great sea battles have put the Japs into reverse, they have lost a large part of their Navy, and without the Navy they now no longer pose a threat to Australia their intended objective. When the American General Mac Arthur was forced out by the Japenese he said "I shall return", and he has, with the material to do the job, it is now the turn of the Jap's to die, They will remember Pearl Harbour.

We in this country are feeling much more enthusiast we have stood with our backs to the wall, just having to stand and take it so badly prepared were we, and it is not in a Britisher's make up to do that, he responds immediatly if he has the means to do it, now we have.

A bit of excitment today, one of our ATC officers has arranged a visit to a local Canadian Airfield, seems the Canadian C O is a drinking partner of officer Alex, anyhow the guy has sent a truck for us, and the two Canadian's seem as pleased as we were.

Great guys these Canadians, but they get rather bored if they have very little to interest them. They came over here to fight but cooped up in an Army camp in Aldershot was a little more than they could stand, What really triggered it I don't know but a number of them, probably after a few drinks went into Aldershot and knocked hell out of it, I don't suppose the people of Aldershot thought much of it but any soldier would understand their frustration.

Well we are here now, what a feeling standing on a real airfield (with permission), Hello guy's says the fella with ginger hair and moustache, my name is Ruane, if no one is around I am known as ginger, this guy is Otto, he is called that because he comes from Ottawa, and he is forever on about it. Otto was a young man around 21 years old, not many years older than our eldest cadet, but he has his "wings" and for what came next that was just as well.

We were taken to a large open ended structure of corrugated Iron and had our first feel of a real aircraft. Right you can sit in it but keep your paws of those buttons, how does it feel?, got plenty of space, fit your bum in alright? and we all laughed. What a feeling, we were sitting where real pilots had sat.

Now said Ginger with a look of absolute glee on his face, I have an hour too spare and Otto and I are going to take you up for a spin no more than 10 minutes and not that if the Gerry's arrive, then you will be down pronto. I think the grin on his face said it all, he saw on our faces what he had expected to see excitment mixed with fear, we had only come to see the airfield. But we were certainly not going to refuse, this was something any boy would give his years ration of sweets for!

The Canadians were great fighters but tended to do their own thing, and one by one Ginger and Otto gave us the thrill of our lives.

They would have known we would be shaking with fearful excitement and I suspect they would be having a smile at our expense, but not one of us would have missed it for the world.

I would think it was really against the rules, but as I have said Canadians are not ones for too much yes sir, no sir, and I think their top brass knew that and kept the "bull shine" to a minimum.

Well guys how was it||? we left Ginger and Otto in no doubt as to what we felt, it was fantastic. Glad you liked the show and I hope one day you will all get your "wings". I have to go now, and if we meet again I hope it is Canada, I also come from Ottawa, so just ask for Ginger and we all laughed at the thought of Ginger among a few million Canadians.

Last stop was the canteen for dinner, as we made our way there every guy seemed to have a grin, I guess it was the sight of these "boys" in uniform that would have looked a little amusing and perhaps they had boys back home.

In keeping with their reputation for hospitality we came away well satisfied, we had had all we could eat and drink.

As we walked pass the cooks, dishing i tout we made a point of a "thanks guys" for each one and received a grin that went from ear to ear. What a day! now our truck is waiting. We did not expect to se him again but Ginger has roared up in his jeep, All the best guys, glad you enjoyed your visit, keep your heads down, Oh and tell that crafty Coyoty Alex that tonight *all* the drinks are on him.

What a day indeed, I think now all the learning of the morse code, aircraft recognition, marching and saluting are all well worth while, for a couple of evenings a week. Still I cannot help wondering about Ginger's remarks about officer Alex.

Crafty Coyote, drinks are *all* on him with the emphasis on the all. Firstly Officer Alex had a "very important appointment" in London, then that unexpected flight, the absolute glee with which Ginger announced it, he could see on our faces the very look he had expected, excited apprension, and his grin widened, I think Alex and Ginger had some kind of bet, and we were the meat in the sandwich, no matter, drink up Alex here's to you, we have had a fantastic day and I think Ginger and Otto have too, heres to Canada!

After that great day out, life at work seems even more boring, just spraying a dull grey green paint on vehicles for the ministry of aircraft production I am beginning to look forward to my call up papers, however a slight variation today but not very exciting.

We have an older fella here probably in his mid fifties, not a bad chap, the worst thing about him is he sings songs of the 1920s all day, it does not really bother us it just makes a bit of a joke at times and makes a laugh, He has a stiff leg brought about by a piece of shell shrapnel in the 14-18 war, so today's happening was a little provoking to say the least.

The governor is a little careful with his money, but his wife is down right mean, she has told old Joe that she had paid him one halfpenny too much this week, but she will make it right next week. When Joe told us we just had to laugh, it was so dreadfully mean, but the old boy was not laughing he was quite the reverse, usually, very quiet. I thought of the song often on the radio, There will always be an England, one of the lines is "this worth fighting for", I feel at that moment Joe would have had his doubts.

Monday today, not a good day at the best of times, tempers can flare up easily and today one did. Don was a very quiet chap and very good at his job, but somewhat lacking in humour. He sat on his box, brush and pallets in his hands writing a sign board taking very little notice of anyone else.

A young apprentice found this a little amusing and was flicking drops of water at Don "cut that out" said Don, the apprentice was now quite pleased to see Don getting a little agitated and increased the amount. The next thing was Don placed his brush down carefully picked up Eddy's bucket and poured the whole lot over him, Eddy was soaked, the rest of us were splitting our sides with laughter the best laugh we had had for a very long time, but at that moment a thought went through my mind, what if we were under German occupation. A German guard with his gun over his shoulder would have quickly been on the scene, Achtung, Acttung, back to vork, back to vork, and we would have had to obey him, and a grin came back on my face, you know mate ,this is worth fighting for! Many under German occupation are forced to work for them at the barrel of a gun.

Christmas is here again and one of the good things about it is, we get three days peace, the Germans also celebrate christmas. It is an odd thought we kill each other every day but we pray to the same God, but I don't doubt there are just as many Germans as Britons who pray for an end to the war.

Tonight the church will be full again, as it is every christmas, everyone will be praying for someone, perhaps somebody whose life hangs in the balance, somebody who has just received the telegram from the War Office telling them "regret your son is missing, presumed dead", maybe anothers son has been torpedod and his ship sunk, maybe he managed to get a life raft, it will be many days before she will know, but she has her faith in God and life will be bearable.

Christmas dinner is about the same, plenty of vegetables a whaco lump of Pork from Bill's governor, from a pig that the Ministry of Food never got to hear about. Mum's cherry brandy rounds off the day, and so to bed, not very exciting perhaps but we are still here, HAPPY CHRISTMAS!.

We have had many bombs on the town, but yesterday was the worst air raid we have had. The raids we get now are what are termed as "Hit and Run" raids, the German's come in at roof top height, drop their bombs and are on their way back across the Channel before thr RAF can get them.

In the past we would have had an air raid warning of about 20 minutes, with the hit and run this is reduced to 20-30 seconds leaving almost no time to take cover. Yesterday's was just such a raid, I was at work when the "spotters warning" sounded. The spotter men were on high points who on actualy seeing the enemy planes would sound the warning, obviously there were only seconds before they were with us, and as they came in with their machine guns blazing I did not feel too safe in my corrugated roofed building.

There was of course nothing one could do, as the raid would be over in a couple of minutes, you either copped it or thought yourself lucky. They roared over the town at roof top height, t his noise was enough, but the bombs they dropped produced a feeling of absolute terror, with more noise, and shaking building this corrugated iron building sounded like it had a troop of dancers on it, Then that awful feeling if I am still here in one piece, who is not.

The Governor, Erne and Fred are Air Raid Wardens, and are half way out the door, Huck the governor said they have dropped one on Godinton Road, you had better get off home. Now I was scared, and it was down Bank Street along Godinton Road as fast as I could pedal, but only as far as the Stanhay Works where the road was covered in slates, glass, asbestos sheeting, and goodness knows what.

Two Air Raid wardens, a young one and an older fella stood with their backs to me, as I passed, the younger one called out hey, where are you going? this area is dangerous, go back. This was just too much, I screamed at him, I know! I know! that is my house round that corner, and that is where I am dam well going. It's alright Jim said the older one, he is one of the Hawn boys, away you go lad.

    I continued to pick my way through the rubble muttering to myself about "little Hitlers" but I had to give that little Hitler a couple of points as I heard him say in a very soft voice to the older one, are they alright?. Yes said the older chap, but the house is a mess. The scene was of absolute devastation, no glass in the windows on either side of the road, it was laying in the road with the slates from the roof I turned down the path to the gate, I did'nt have to open it just walk over it, in the yard was more glaSS more slates and a nasty crack running down the wall.

    No need to open the back door there was'nt one, but as I approached, Dad appeared, hello Dad you alright? and he grinned, course I am Son, that's good, where is Mum? she is in there he said she is alright but badly shocked. I lifted my heavy foot up the step into the living room, what an awful sight, glass again, broken furniture, the ceiling that was above me when I had breakfast, was now on the floor, and there sat Mum her arms rested on a patch of the table where the plaster from the colapsed ceiling had been brushed away.

    She looked up at me, did a bit of a grin and said alright Son? never mind me, how are you Mum? Dad and I are both OK, just hope we all are, I knew she was worried about the three younger ones, and Bill and Herby. I cleared a chair and sat down beside her, well Dad where do we start? We are not starting anywhere until I have had another cup of tea, I don't care if I use up my whole tea ration The tea ration was 2 onces a week, and the way he was going he would do just that, and use ours as well.

Dad went to fill the kettle, I looked at Mum, she was red eyed and still shaking I felt decidedly useless I must do something I thought. We boys were not given to shows of affection, ours was a dog eat dog sort of life, stand on your own two feet, stiff upper lip and all that, but this situation needed something else.

I slid my arm around her, and she promptly burst into tears, and I joined her, the whole thing was a bit too much even for a bi big boy of fifteen years. At that moment the door bell rung I'll answer it Mum, and off I went while rubbing my eyes on my shirt sleeves. At the door was one of the air raid wardens, hello lad ,would you tell your Mum that we will have a tarpaulin over the roof by tonight, the builders are a little busy but they hope they will have a cover over all the worst roofs before dark. Thanks mate I said, sorry I flew off the handle, that's alright Son I would have done the same thing, and he was off to the lady next door. My feelings for air raid wardens have improved.

Mum and Dad were very relieved about the roof, if it rained at that moment it would be the last straw, we can at the moment sweep up the mess, but if it was soaked with rain it would be another story.

After he had drunk his tea, the leader of men could be seen in Dad, right he said Huck, would you help me re-hang the door, and then go up to the pie shop and get something for dinner, I shall then make a start upstairs. I think we need to get the bedroom cleared first, as we shall have no light up there after dark, these curtains can be nailed on a frame to make a black out for this window, and to keep some of the wind out.

I'll make a start upstairs said Mum, are you sure you are up to it Violet? asked Dad, course I am said Mum, and I think doing something was best to take her mind off things. All went as Dad had planned and by dark the inside of the house was tidy, and the builders were as good as their word the roof had a large tarpaulin over it, so no rain could get in. The house itself was still a mess, but in this room we felt secure.

When the schools felt it was safe the children were allowed to go home, and Mum was overjoyed to see them, just Bill and Herby to come.

Bill and Herby have now arrived home, "cor blimey" what happened says Bill, he never got an answer just a great big hug from Mum, she was on her feet with one arm each around Bill and Herby, now we are all here thank good she said and as grim as the situation was it was a room full of smiles.

More tea and we all sat down, well Dad what really happened this morning to cause all this? Well he said I heared this roar of engine noise and machine gun fire, I rushed to the back door but before I could turn the handle the door was on top of me.

What really happened was that as the German plane was approaching it was hit by a machine gunner on a tower a short distance away, it had not released it's bomb, the bomb exploded and the blast from the explosion did maximum damage. The worst of the damage was done to the Stanhay Factory over which it was passing just at the back of our house. There were several people killed one of these was a teenage girl, the damage to our house seemed so unimportant compared to these deaths.

Well we are mentally and physically absolutly tired out, and we vote for bed hoping each of us has cleared the beds thoroughly, it will be a really healthy night with no glass in the windows, but I doubt if anyone will notice that.

The next day we learned of other peoples fates, next in the German's path was Haywards Garage, this was totally destroyed with more deaths, near the garage was a bakers shop also destroyed with more deaths. The main target was probably the Railway Works, where several bombs were dropped and more killed, in all about 50 died. It could have been so much worse if the children of a school in Beaver Road had not been in the shelters when their school received a direct hit, and was totally destroyed, that was our worst day one we will always remember.

The younger children are at home today, and I have wandered down the garden and as I looked across at that factory I was devastated, I turned and looked up at our houses, what a mess, my eyes went down on the garden, this did not help a lot, there on the ground were pieces of human flesh and a crumpled cigarette lighter. These pieces of a human body might have been from the factory or the German pilot, but even if it had been the pilot I could not have raised any kind of a cheer, it was an awful thought that this had been a human being, regardless of nationality.

Today it is like another world. it is a warm spring day, and I have decided to clean up the garden in case the younger ones were to see those remains. I have dug a hole in the garden and placed those remains with the lighter in it, whether they were English or German made no difference I could only say "rest in peace" and really mean it. From that grim task I now stand with the sun on my back looking down at a patch of crocus, some flattened by the blast some fully open soaking up the sun. Twenty yards behind them is our row of houses looking more derelict than habitable, and I thought of those that were killed, and those who waited for those who did not come home, they would look at those crocus but would only see the image of those they had lost, it would be a long time before time, that great healer had done it's work.

Hello Huck said Dad, I think Mum was worried and wondered how or where I was and had asked Dad to come down. I told him I had placed those remains in the ground, and thought I would do a bit of gardening, I think I will move those bluebells over there Dad, I Would'nt do that Son it is almost their time to flower, of course I said it is, that would not do at all I said. Dinner in about 10 minutes, and off he went, he will say to Mum, he is ok Vi, Dad did not worry a lot.

Dad's point about the bluebells made me think of all those that will not bloom this year, they are under thousands of tons of war material, guns, ammunition, tanks, men and huts to house them. This massive build up of material now occupies most forest and woodlands, it must be kept out of sight of German aircraft, they must not know the amount, or where it will be delivered, or when.

The area around here now sounds like a carpenters work shop hammers, drills, and saws, the occasional tinkling of glass, the builders are doing a great job, and the houses are looking a little more habitable. Our house was severly damaged but our family is undamaged, and we think of the undamaged home, with permantly damaged family where one or more will never come home again. None of us will ever forget such tragedy but now and again I permit myself a slight grin when I remember how I shouted at the young air raid warden, and the older one saying it's alright Jim he is one of the Hawn boy's. It was like a rubber stamp on my passport, one of the few occasions I was glad that the Hawn boy's were quite well known.

We were well known not because of our behaviour, but because we were such a large family seven boys and our sister Rita. Not one of us ever saw the inside of a law court, though this might to some degree have been due to the efforts of one of our policemen. He was about six and a half feet tall, and weighed about twenty stone, we called him Tiny, if he caught us up to mischief he would give us a good talking too, and his rather large hand would skim the top of our head probably taking a few hairs with it, and tell us just where to go.

He was a policeman of long ago, one of the parts of his talk would be the shame we could bring on our family, today of course this would not mean a great deal, but to the Hawn boys of those days it certainly did. It was of course a very different form of policing in those days. The policeman would not roar up in his patrol car, he would probably be on foot pushing his cycle and if he caught us up to no good there would be no point in running away because he knew all the local lads anyway, and would soon be round to see Mum.

We had great respect for our police in the war, we relied on them more for problems brought about by the war more than we did for crime. It was very reassuring to see them after that air raid in all the chaos it meant order would be restored as soon as possible, and there was that other duty when they would have to visit the unfortunate relatives of the dead and injured, when the constable would have to say "I am very sorry Mam but I----- We had a visit from our policeman after that raid, but fortunatly not for that reason. Our policemen were quite friendly but boys still had a feeling of "look out it's a copper" when we saw one, so when I answered the door to one is scared the pants off me. Hello Son you alright? made a bit of a mess did'nt they still we have got them on the run now they won't do this again, Is your Mum in? yes I said with great relief.

We had got them on the run, they could not run fast enough in North Africa, the eighth army under General Montgomery, with the American army behind them had the German Afrika Korp in a position of no escape. The invincible German war machine in this case the Africa Korps under Field Marshall Rommel has surrendered, Rommel himself has escaped, he will live to fight another day, and Hitler is sure going to need him.

The oil that this war machine needs still lies in Iran and Iraq the closest they got was Egypt.

The German Afrika Korps might have got it, but not now, and the oil of Russia will soon be out of their reach, as the Russian advance continues. It is a marvellous feeling we always knew we would win, now it's just a matter of when.

In our darkest hour at the start of the war our position seemed almost impossible, but we did have the free world behind us, Germany and it's cities are being pounded into rubble, they will know that the *world* is against them and that Winston Churchill's demand of unconditional surrender is all that we will accept, we were sure we would win, but the German people will know that after their homes, and people have been blown to bits they will have fought and died for nothing. One can only hope that never again will they go to war, and Europe will live in peace.

We in this country feel a different people, all around the world we advance, we do not retreat, we attack, we do not just defend. We are really moving and we have the means.

The Afrika Korps surrendered in May, and in July our forces were in Sicily, it was a difficult fight but victory was soon ours, and now on the anniversary of the out break of the war September 3rd 1939 our forces are in Italy, mainland Europe. It's a great feeling but we think of our men .In keeping the dislike the Italians have for war, they surrendered as soon as we landed in their country leaving their allies Germany to face the inevitable mass distruction that was to come.

If the Italians thought they could save themselves from this fate they were of course very much mistaken, the German's saw the surrender as cowardice and an act of betrayal and every inch of Italian soil would be fought over, not to defend Italy, but to delay any entry into Germany.

We have no love for Germany but find that situation rather disgusting, in the early days of the war the Italians were right behind Hitler's Germany because it appeared to be at that time the Winning side. To give the Italians a couple of points they did relieve Mussolini from command of the Italian war machine, but as our forces had almost captured Sicily less than 10 miles from Italy, it did appear to be more a desperate attempt at self preservation.

We in Britain had been in a very similar situation in 1940 but surrender was never mentioned, and never would be, until the situation was absolutly impossible and we could fight no more. I think at the time it was the only thing we had in common with the German's.

We now have a family interest in the Italian war zone, brother Les and cousin Monty are now there and we are of course very concerned. Cousin Monty is an R S M (regimental sargent major) The RSM is the scourge of the parade ground. He loves the sound of his own voice, he will call the new recruits all manor of abusive names, he knows that the regimental routine will protect him. He will have them marching round the parade grounds with all equipment on their backs no matter what the temperature or time. From his position in the shade he will bellow out, we will get it right if I have to stand here till dark, the only part of him that would over heat was his tongue, unlike his victims.

The men to show their fondness for him have chrisened him Gobshite, he has probably got to hear of his new name and I expect he is delighted that he has had the desired effect on the men.

On the battlefield the R S M would be the guy you would want to have around, and those days on parade ground would quickly be forgotten. Although he was of "questionable parentage" he was after all more one of us than one of them, and the men would be much more confident following him than the new officer fresh out of training college where he would have been taught the basic rules, but it is on the battlefield where a man learns just what war is, and Monty has learnt a lot, he must have been rather amused to be Monty the same as the eighth army General Montgomery. Monty was a good soldier and knew what was good for the regiment, and more importantly what was good for him.

Our forward troops are doing well and Monty's unit has just arrived and are welcomed with open arms, literaly, and one of those giving this welcome was a very nice young lady who was not slow in spotting this rather nice tall, dark and handsome soldier obviously not an ordinary private. The young lady's name was Rosa, and Monty was not slow in improving this image that Rosa had of him, and soon had romance blossoming, this was probably helped by a few items from the cook house for Rosa's family, food being a little short.

In those days Italian Mums and Dads would keep an eye on the progress of such a romance, but progress it did and eventually Monty brought Rosa to England.

All went well for a good number of years, but sadly Rosa died long before she was an old lady. She died while still a very lovely person, lively, slim and pleasent, we were all saddened by he her death. In between meeting Rosa and bringing her to England Monty's unit had too move on, but before he did he got to know that brother Les was in the same area and took him to meet Rosa and her family, a meeting much enjoyed by all, it was great to be with a civilian family in amongest the devastation of war.

Les is on an airfield with the R A F supplying air cover for the troops up front, air support is absolutly necessary for a successful operation.

Today Les having prepared and cooked the meal, he is on the bench dishing it out, not the cooks favourite job, they don't mind but some of the remarks are not too flattering, today is no exception. The guy has just received his dinner when he makes some insulting remarks about it, Les quickly responds. Look mate, I don't buy it, or grow it, they just give it to me, I cook it and you have got it now move along. Unfortunatly the guy behind Mr Abnoxious is the camp clown Chalky White, and having had the queue warmed up by the previous guy he set about getting a few laughs. What is it he asks in a nice loud voice knowing he would get a laugh and a cheer from the queue. I don't know, I have not named it yet say's Les, the words were a little unfortunate and Chalky quickly seized his chance, again in a nice loud voice said, slightly turning to the queue, AH I think I can help you there mate, more cheers from the rear and Chalky is about to take a bow when his act is cut short.

The duty officer sees Les about to vault over the serving bench and in a commanding voice that had obviously been building up for some minutes, orders, that man! take your dinner, find a table and eat it, or leave the dining area NOW, you could have heard a pin drop, Chalky looked a little sheepish, Les had a beaming smile and order once more was restored.

This particular officer had crossed swords with Les in the past and knew that while Les was good at his job, he also had a short fuse, and did not suffer idiots too well. It was no good an officer throwing his weight around in the cookhouse, even if he was an Air Vice Marshal, he would know that as an army "marches on it's stomach" so the RAF flies on it's stomach, there is no better way to get unrest on a camp than messing up the food supply. Stupid orders from junior officers straight from training college would do just that, however, every man has the right to complain to the duty officer, in the proper manner, if he has a complaint about his meal.

Back in the army General Montgomery's eighth army has had to reduce it's rate of progress, the reason being the Monastry on the top of the next hill. The Monastry is a beautiful building it is most imposing, with the Monks it presented no problem, but the German's have moved in and it could now be a fortress.

General Montgomery has a reputation for not risking his men's lives, the 14-18 idea of war where men were hurled at enemy machine guns is fortunatly long gone, and so there is an agonizing discussion going on as to what to do about this building that is slowing our advance. This building with its vital position is pinning our troops down for miles around. Montgomery and his opposite American number must decide it's fate. Orders were given to destroy the Monastry.

Italy is a land of rivers, and hills, and ideal for defenders, but not for an advancing army, anything "man made" that holds up that advance must be destroyed. I think much has been learned from the 14-18 war, instead of throwing men at fortified positions our leaders have landed the army up the coast at Anzio behind the present front line, it was never the less touch and go.
The Germans did their best to push our men back into the sea, but we held on and it was successful.

Not far away was Rome it has now been occupied by our troops, they are now about 600 miles from the first landing, if it were not for the difficult terain they might have doubled that.
It is certainly a defenders country, and the German's are fighting for every inch of Italian soil as if it was German, they know that over that mountain Range to the north it is German.

Our Russian allies are rolling their German enemy back, this invincable German war machine is in reverse, it cannot stop. The Russians will roll it back too the gates of Berlin.

German morale is collapsing, orders from Hitler expressively forbidding retreat are being ignored, two years ago they might have fought to the last man, but not now. From his bunker in Berlin he would issue such orders as he had in the past, but his Gererals though they are first rate soldiers are not willing to throw battle weary men against a superior Russian Army. A counter attack which they knew would fail ,they too have learnt from the 14-18 war.

In the far east it is the same story, our armies are taking back the islands lost to the Japanese, each island is one nearer Japan, and one further away from their objective Australia. They now also see the begining of the end.

In Burma it is we that advance not they. The Japs had their greedy eyes on the Indian frontier, and it was getting closer, but now it grows further away, where ever German, Jap, Italian leaders look, they see the same inevitable end, unconditional surrender.

What a change in our people, those backs too the wall days of 1940, having to just stand and take all that the Germans could drop on us, seeing our army retreat across France, The French surrender, the realization that we stood alone with very little too fight back with, now we have it, and how we will use it.

We did of course have that valiant victory of the RAF, The Battle of Britain, that I think was a saviour in more ways than one, strategically, and morrally, these valiant young men of the RAF kept our heads above water, it seemed impossible at the time, the odds were so stacked against them, but they did it.

Now yet again the tables have turned, more and more raids are being made on German cities, often made by 1000 plus aircraft, such a raid recently dropped 2500 tons of bombs on Berlin. It is obvious that the death and distruction must be devastating, but to a country at war revenge is sweet. It is not possible to feel any pity for a country that has inflicted so much pain and suffering on the world. It is an eye for an eye, tooth for a tooth, as ye sow, so then ye shall reap.

A German may well remember pre war day's when the flags flew, the massive rallies of storm troopers, the military bands with their nationalistic music, the threats to other countries Hitler thumping the the table in front of him, and promising that the disgrace of the 1918 surrender at Versailes would be avenged. Now to a German it is becoming clear that all he can expect was another defeat, but this time bearing no resemblance to 1918 this time his country would be devastated beyound belief, we all hope he will choose war no more.

Today is 6th June 1944, this is a day that nobody in this country will ever forget, D DAY.
This Island has been almost sinking under the weight of every kind of war material needed for the war, and thousands of men from many different nations from around the world. Now this equipment and these men are taking part in the greatest invasion ever known, the forces of the free world have landed in France.

This is what the people of Russia have wanted for so long, now Hitler must fight on two fronts and in the process take some of the heat off our ally Russia. All night long the air has been filled with the sound of aircraft, loaded with thousands of tons of bombs for the German defences. Other aircraft are towing gliders filled with troops, these gliders will be released from the aircraft and glide to earth hoping to miss the trees and maybe the odd greenhouse, or chicken hut, they will then hold the more important objectives until the main forces arrive.

The navy has also been softening up the shore defences, it is estimated that approximately 600 big guns from the fleet have been pounding the German's, under this terrific bombardment our troops are going ashore.

It is almost impossible to imagine what these men are thinking they will walk up these beaches carrying their equipment facing any fortifications still intact, with every gun that the German army can train upon them. None will turn around, and shell fire will drown the screams of their wounded comrades and nobody will question their orders, they will all be well aware of their objectives and of course one always thinks, it will be the other guy that gets it, not me.

There were of course many killed and wounded, but it would have been many times worse if the German's had known just where the invasion would come, it is thought the German's were expecting it at the shorter distance of Dover, Calais and not Normandy as it was.

The radio continually reports on the progress of our forces not so much the resistance they were meeting, but we don't need to know that, it is not difficult to imagine, sheer hell I should think.

These men have trained and retrained for every conceivable situation, in all kinds of weather, couped up in army camps it might even be a relief to get going.

This is day two and our forces are moving inland, now every German available will be moved up to face them and progress will be difficult, the order from Hitler is no retreat, the allies must be thrown back into the sea, but it is too late there can only be one outcome to this momentous battle, this invasion force is here to stay.

The people in Britain have been glued to every news bulletin and in their minds have had the end of the war not far away, but hardly had we finished cheering than we were presented with another very nasty problem.

It is a grey cloudy day, very low cloud and I am at work the time is about 8-3o, the other men have gone out on their jobs and as the boss has not yet arrived it means I am here on my Jack Jones. This is quite OK, not unusual, but what is very unusual is the noise of the objects passing overhead, they are coming over every few minutes each one has the sound of several car engins without silencers, and I have never heard anything like it. I have gone outside to the road hoping somebody would know what was going on, but all were in the same boat as me, nobody knew what these terrifying objects were.

The most awful thing about it was because of the low cloud we could not see a thing, it was a little frightening, but we knew it must be German and it would almost certainly be carrying a large amount of explosives, and as we heard no explosion it was probably on its way to London. To say the least it was somehow rather scarey, and it was with some relief that I heard the governor come in.

Morning Huck, don't like the sound of these things, do you? I have just been told what they are, they are Hitler's latest weapon, Flying Bombs, or V1 weapons as the German's call them.

The German's are launching them on a course to London, they have enough fuel to get them there and then a mechanical device will operate to send them down on London where the explosive war head will detonate, just before it falls the engine will stop, if you heard it stop you would know that you had just seconds to find a hole.

This new weapon must be Adolf Hitler's last throw of the dice he is again gambling on creating such terror in London that the people will crack, it seems he has learnt nothing.

He will be well aware of the situation in Normandy, the battle for the French town of Caen has been extremly difficult, the Germans have shown great determination to throw us back into the sea as Hitler had ordered, but it is too late the town has fallen to the British, and Canadian troops. There will be no retreat now. There has never been such an awesome array of war material, of fighting men, and machines as there is in Normandy today. Adolf Hitler may well reflect on the ambitions as he might have had.

It has been said he planned world domination, governed by pure German stock, tall, blond, blue eyes Arians, and they would be called the master race. The gypsies, Jews, the sub normal anyone who did not come up to the standard would be a burden on the state, and no doubt Hitler would know how to rectify that situation.

Had he studied history a little more he would have realised that the chance of permanant domination of one country by another was virtually nil.

It has also been said that he had a great admiration for the British Empire, perhaps that is what he dreamed of. Of course at that time he would not have known that our Empire as such would cease to exist in the years too come.

In this day and age it would be totally immoral to try to suppress the will of any people on earth, today, of course Hitler had no such feelings he did I think see the rest of the world as lazy, decadent people who would readily submit to his war machine.
He had no respect whatever for our prime minister at that time .However when Winston Churchill took command it was quite a different story, he was left in no doubt that we would fight, and as Churchill said we would never surrender.

No doubt Churchill would have been on Hitler's list for extermination and Churchill would have known that, and at the time, Hitler might have got his way, but it did not stop Churchill calling Hitler some very nasty names.

Churchill would have known just how weak we wre Militarly but every one of his speeches put fire in our bellies, when he said no surrender, that was the way it would be. I think Hitler still hoped to do a deal with Britain, but I am sure it would not have been worth the paper it was written on.

No chance of a deal now the going is tough, but progress is good, our invasion of France has I feel gone according to plan. Churchill and General Eisenhower chose the landing area well, the Normandy Peninsula was very difficult to defend, and now it has fallen we have a large port where we can land the thousands of tons of equipment that we will need before the war ends.

The flying bombs are a problem as they are faster than our spitfires but the RAF has got them in their sights, by keeping fighters in the air along their route it, is just a question of waiting for one to come along. A few bursts of cannon fire sends a great number of them to earth, but unfortunatly while each one is one less for London, it is one more for us down below, when we heared the engin stop we knew that in less than a minute there is going to be an explosion not far away.

The anti-aircraft guns also have a go and it is quite a sight seeing black shell bursts all around the bomb as it falls through the air, but their success was not great and it is thought that some of the damage in the town was caused by AA shells falling to earth.

The flying bomb (V1) was soon followed by (V2) this was a rocket fired from a launching pad in France, it would soon reach a height where it would not be seen or heard until the unfortunate Londoner felt the explosion of it's 2000 lb of explosive. This was really nerve shattering but our invasion forces eventualy over ran the launching sights, plus they received a great deal of attention from the RAF, but knowing the people of London it must have been a very nasty period. especially not knowing when one would arrive.

Progress is now much better in Italy, Monty and Les are both O K but we are always very concerned for their safety, it is a hell of a country to fight in, just too many hills and rivers.

Thr Russians have streamed across their own country and Poland and are now only 400 miles from Berlin, I am sure they have plans for Hitler when they get there.

The Japs were getting closer to brother Ern, but now they get further away as they retreat in Burma.

All around the world wherever we fight the writing is on the wall for our enemies, few will escape ,most of the leaders will be hung by the neck until they are dead.
Of course we are still some months from victory, but things are a little more relaxed, air raids are now not very likely as the German's need every aircraft on the other side of the channel in Italy and on the Russian front.

Food does not change a lot, it is still very difficult feeding our 45 million people. Shipping cannot be spared for avacardos or pomegranates, hand grenades, guns etc., are a little more important. Bananas are sometimes flown to Britain, but only for hospital patients, whose condition can be helped by them, all we see is a picture in the paper of a nice hand of bananas, in black and white of course.

Mum also seems a little more relaxed, she has two sons in war zones but she only has Derek and Rita at school now, the older ones are able to look after themselves.

Most of my work is now painting RAF lorries with khaki drab paint, no job satisfaction here just boredom. The colour has gone out of the job, as all the good quality paint has long been used up, paint or what goes under the name of paint is now made from fish oil.

In a few months time I shall be called up for the services I don't know which one. I hope it will be the RAF, but two of our best air cadets have had to join the army.
The war ministry have told us that there are no positions in the RAF all men of eighteen will now be placed in the army, it seems a rotten trick after all the work we have done in the air training corps. If the governor gets his way I might not get away, he thinks he might get me off by applying for reserved occupation status, I sure hope he fails.

Today is September 3rd, the anniversary of the outbreak of war, surely this must be the last one, it really does look like it with our forces and the Russians making such good progress. Soon all the death and distruction will be on German soil, those who started the war should have their fair share, unfortunatly the French, Belgians and Dutch have suffered badly before we could get at the Germans. We have been feeling great with our armies doing so well, but today we are rather quiet.

Around 8000 airborne men, and men in gliders have been dropped into the area around Arnhem, their job was to stop the Germans blowing the bridges, they were too hold them until the main force arrived, but the Germans threw all they had against them. When only 2000 were still in a condition to fight it was decided they must pull out. It is difficult to image the hammering that they took, it failed, but they will be remembered for their great gallantry and sacrifice.

Christmas day, this also surely must be the last one before the war ends, some of the troops have been fighting for nearly six years, we all hope they will be home for christmas 1945.

It is an awful thought that when they do get home their younger children will not know them. One can only imagine this man standing in the doorway, mummy will throw her arms around him, he will hug her as to almost crush her. Mummy will call to little Tommy, come quickly Daddy is here, but little Tommy will see only a man that he has never seen before.

Dad will try hard to make friends he would so love to pick Tommy up and give him a great big hug, but Dad will know that this may take a few days. Tommy holds tight to Mummy's skirt and tears fill the eyes of both Mum and Dad, this little boy is the baby that Dad has never held in his arms, those precious years are gone, they will work hard to make up what they have lost.

What of the man home from the war || who has known only army routine, obey every order, question none, this man will now have to be a father to young Tommy a little boy who has known only the love of his Mummy, he could so easily become a souce of friction between his Mum and Dad.
That of course is some way off.
Our troops are moving forward at a good rate, and the RAF and USAF are pounding the German's continually, whether it be troop concentrations or German cities.
German towns and cities are becoming just skeletons with piles of rubble. London, Coventry and all other towns and cities of Britain that have been bombed without mercy are being avenged with interest.

Today I have a day off from work, I have received my call up papers and I have to go to Maidstone for a medical examination to see if I am fit for service in the Army or RAF. I expect it wil be the army as the ATC boys who have already gone were placed in the army, a bit tough really.

Well here I am, there a lot of lads about my age and we are sent into a room and told to be quiet. Now in walks a man in uniform who bellows out right on your feet! you will now remove all your cloths, all of them || asks one lad, all of them say's the guy enjoying every minute.

He has before him boys who have never been in a situation that resembled anything like it, and he as going to make the most of it. When your name is called you will go through those doors where you will find a number of doctors who will examine you, after which you will report to me, is that clear? nobody answered but we got the message.

As our names were called in alphabettical order a number had gone in, that is my name so in I go.

I opened the door and went in, and there was a sight I shall always remember, all around this very large hall were cubicles with a doctor in each, and at each one stood a very young man completly nude (not a stich on)

Having quite a good sense of humor I just had to laugh, not a very good start I think, the first doctor took hold of a part of my anatomy and said cough, not something the average young man had experienced, after about a dozen doctors had checked every bit of me I was able to leave the hall of doctors, and having dressed report to the beaming guy at the desk.

Right that is all, you will be hearing in about a fortnight and with another snigger we were out of the door. In a couple of weeks I will get a letter telling me where to go to join the army it is almost certain it will not be the RAF, I am a bit niggled about that, but it has got to be more exciting than spraying paint.

The way things are going it could be all over before I get in, most of our army is now up to the West Bank of the Rhine, and the East Bank is being bombed continously in preparation for the river being crossed. A group of men have settled down for the night in a convienient bomb crater, they have about 4 hours to day light and must get some sleep. It would be unwise to be asleep after day break, one might just never wake up again.

Like most soldiers the last thing one thinks of before going to sleep is the family back home, wife, children, home, garden, even bells across the meadow, everything that they hold dear, and so to sleep.

It is not quiet, but not too bad, the flashes and the rumble of bombs are about 10 miles away, our aircraft never let up, it goes on all the time. It must be hell to live in Germany just now.

When our Generals are satisfied that the East Bank fortification have more or less been wiped out the men will be going over, some by a nice firm bridge, and some on a pontoon bridge, assembled by the Royal Engineers.

About 5 miles in from the East bank sits "Karl", also in a bomb crater, there are plenty to go round. He must now fight with his back to the wall and try to put off the inevitable end. He might hope that there will be an armistice, but in the back of his mind like most German's he knows those words of Churchill Unconditional Surrender mean just that, no deal.

Karl will be well aware that his fatherland is being systematically destroyed, every town which has any kind of military potential is being reduced to rubble. He will also be aware of the fact that for the Unconditional Surrender to be brought about ,every metre of German soil must be over run by allied troops until they meet the Russian army from the east.

At some point his family, Mother, Brother and Sister will meet the enemy that are soon to flood across the Rhine, and he might hope they will be treated a little better than some of the people that have been under German occupation. Karls family will be a little more fortunate than some that are about to receive the Russians.

The Russians have much more to repay, many thousands murdered by his German comrades, somebody has to pay.

It is a little ironic that when his idol Adolph Hitler plunged the world into this murderous war, Karl was about 12½ years old. the same age as myself. Amid all the flag waving, rally's and rabble raising speeches he joined the Hitler youth, they gave him a uniform, took him to great rallies, he listened to the great man Adolph issuing his threats, thumping the desk and the future of the fatherland was assured.

Now this boy of 17½ has answered his Furhers call and is a German soldier. He is Hitler's ideal German, blond, blue eyed the very image of a true German arian, a fine specimen of the master race, Hitler's dream. As he lay in his bomb crater he would have known he was in great danger and that the cursed dream of world domination was now in ruins.

As daylight dawns there is another bomb crater very close to Karl's, a much bigger one and it has almost filled in the one that Karl shared with his comrades, of whome there is no trace now.

His mother will be informed, your son has died for the glory of the Fatherland, which she will put with the one she had when her husband was killed, on the Russian front, and as her tears flow, her eyes settle on this fine young man in his smart Hitler youth uniform, he be lieved all that his idol said, and she might say to herself, well I suppose we all did, Did'nt we, and cry again.

As my "appointment || was for 9 o clock in the morning it seemed a good idea to ask Aunty Flo in Lancaster if she could put me up for a couple of days, which she was quite happy to do. Lancaster was rather a long way from Kent. On the day I arrived I met the family and had an enjoyable evening, but that left one whole day before my "appointment", so I thought I would have a day in Blackpool. The day went rather well I met a group of lads and lassies, and lost track of the time and as a result I arrived back at Aunt Flo's at eleven o clock, the house was in darkness. I gently took hole of the door handle, turned it but nothing happened, it was locked. Aunt Flo was a dear old soul, but I could just hear Uncle Jim, a no nonsense sort of guy saying, right lock the door, if he cant get home at a reasonable hour that's his hard luck.

With rather an unknown sort of day tomorrow I could do with a good nights sleep, so I began trying the windows, they were all locked except the small larder window. Not having lived here I could not be sure of the layout inside but there was nothing else for it, in we go. I dangled my foot inside feeling for a firm surface put my weight on it and hoped it would hold me, success, and off to bed.

I was in no hurry to get up in the morning hoping Uncle Jim would have gone to work and give me a chance to make a fuss of Aunty Flo, it all went well, and on my way I go with a whole new life before me. Aunt Flo said Squiresgate used to be a holiday camp before the war, sounded good.

The government says I must report for service with the army (conscription), today's the day.

The entrance did not look much like a holiday camp, there was a soldier on each side of the barrier and a nasty looking bloke in a red hat, with M P on his arm I soon learned that meant military Police.

Name? The red hat says, Hawn I said, right over there and I joined the queue beside H, not much being said, I think we all felt a little apprehensive. We were read the rules and regulations told what would be expected of us in this glorious regiment. The Kings Own. and shown where we would sleep for the next six weeks. We were told where to collect our bedding, uniforms and various other things among which was a couple of metal dishes which were called "mess tins", very well named as these would be our meal plates.

We finally, got to bed having been round that perishing camp a number of time's we were ready for some sleep. The beds were a bit grim but we will get used to it.

There were four of us in this little room, it has a wooden door, at six thirty a.m it is bashed three times by the brass headed batton carried by the C S M (company sargent major) who bawles out right! outside in five minutes. I began to think "you know mate I don't think you should have joined" but then it occured to me that I did not have a lot of choice in the matter. Another day with a dozen things to attend to and we are then told what will happen tomorrow.

You will rise at six thirty, you will wash and shave, sweep the floor of your challet, lay your kit out neatly on your bed, be at the cook house for breakfast and on parade in the main square at seven thirty.

When we got to the square there were four guys obviously variable degrees of superiority, one of which was the guy with the brass stick the C S M.

Right, form three ranks, and we quickly shuffles into three lines as "requested". I will now introduce you to your N C Os who will endeavour to turn you into soldiers during the next six weeks.

April 19th 1945 another day firmly fixed in my mind, the day I joined His Majesties service, namely the army. I am on the station platform at Lancaster railway station on route for Blackpool, the nearest station to my destination Squires gate where all aspects of army life will be revealed to me.

I am your company sergeant major, and it is my job to see that they do, got that? You become first rate soldier.

This is lance corporal Dane.
This is corporal Mc Cann.
This is sergeant Murray.

Each will now tell you precisely what is expected of you to bring about this transformation. When they open their mouths I thought, my luck! One was a geordie from Newcastle, Mc Cann was a Scot from Glasgow, Murray was an Irishman from Belfast. Here I am the only guy from the South, they all have weird accents, none of them speak "Kings English" and I get an international team of instructors, "Gor blimey" well they don't accept resignations so I guess I am stuck with them, roll on six weeks.

One of the guys in my challet is a Scot, he asks whose got the broosh? whose got the broosh? nobody answers, you've got it he says to me, and takes the broom, that is a broom I said, but it was not the time for an English lesson, and we both laughed we were all in the same boat.

Well it is up and down the parade ground marching and saluting and loads of it. I can understand the Irish sergeant and the Newcastle guy, but that Scots corporal sounds like he is from another planet.

They are obviously trying to get us in shape judging by the food. This morning it was a piece of bacon so hard you broke it instead of cutting it, one slice of bread and some porridge, the porridge was probably at the request of that perishing Scotsman Mc Cann.

My international team of instructors, the Scot. the Gordie and the Irishman, tell us that we will be first rate soldiers before they are done with us, (or else) the way it has been up to now I don't think I fancy the "or else".

It is difficult seeing myself measuring up to the standard of our guys in Germany, but that heathen Scotsman does seem very determined.

Those guys in Germany are now over the Rhine and well on their way to Berlin. The opposition from the East Bank was less than expected, the RAF and the USAF had bombed the area unmercifully. One town on the East Bank, Wesel, was virtually obliterated, this was necessary as the German's had heavily fortified the town, the devastation was such that our guy's took only 4 hours to take the town, or what was left of it.

They still have 300 miles to Berlin but it is getting a little easier, the German soldiers are surrendering in their thousands, perhaps they can literally see the inevitable, it could be better to be a live coward than a dead hero.

To be fair that label could not be pinned on either a British or German soldier. The Germans although fighting for the wrong ideals did largely stick to the Geneva convention rules of war. There were of course times when t hey were nothing short of bloody murderes, and this might have helped them surrender, they would know that our troops must inevitably over run the towns of their families and the longer they prolonged the war the more German civillians would die.

They might have hoped to be going home, but they are destined for a long period of time in a British prisoner of war camp.

On the other side of the world our forces fight a very different enemy, the Japanese. The Geneva convention rules of war meant nothing to them. They were cruel sadistic robots, "A death before dishoner army" to surrender was an act of cowardice.
To offer a Japanese the chance to surrender was far too risky they could not be trusted, they had to be killed.

Like their German allies they were slowly being pushed back to Japan, but the jungle fighting is a much slower process, still they too will see how futile it has all been, and some will commit "Hari Kari" and kill themselves rather than go home a prisoner, an awful dishoner.

Back at Squiresgate I think we are making progress aS we have actually got our hands on a rifle. It is quite obvious that most of us have not held one before. When it was waved in the direction of the instructor he was rather annoyed and said some "quite nasty" words.

I was very pleased with my shooting a nd so was my instructor I thought I might make Brigadier yet. I managed to get a two inch group at 300 yards with four shots. For a short while I felt great but then it occured to me what happened to the best shots, they ended up in the Infa ntry, and my shooting deteriorated rapidly, not my idea of a military career.

Having returned from the range with all our equipment on, it gave corporal Mc Cann great pleasure to bawl out right on parade in 5 minutes in P T shorts and singlet, those that did not make it would be on "sand bashing" that evening.

Sqiresgate camp was on sand, and the sand bashers had to sweep it off the road, the wind soon blew it back ready for Mc Cann's victims next day.

Brother Les in Italy is still preparing food for the air crews that bomb the German's every day, the bombs that make the advance of our troops a little easier. Cousin Monty is still with our advance forces up at the sharp end, but their job in Italy is now do ne as the German's there have surrendered, their position was hopeless.

We in Britain are quite excited as it seems that the whole damned thing is nearly over. In less than a fortnight our troops have advanced almost 300 miles, all the main cities have fallen with little resistance. Some German units fight on but they will to continue the war has gone out of the German's, they surrender in their thousands.

It Italy Mussolini and his mistress have been shot by fellow Italians and they now hang upside down for all to see. I don't think I will get to Germany now the end is so near, and Mc Cann seems to have thought the same, he is now concentrating on jungle fighting.
We are crawling on our stomachs in this long grass while he bellows out get your behinds down t hey can be seen for miles. Don't load that rifle with the palm of your hands that might be easier but you could end up dead and so on.
I begin to think where I would like to put that bayonet on the end of my rifle. I wonder if there would be a hissing noise as it went in, he sure is a windbag. Things are getting a little harder, yesterday was tough, and today we have a five mile run in complete uniform, and two packs on our backs, the only good thing is it is with sergeant Murray, and not the Scotsman.

Sergeant Murray is alright, we had not got half way when he called a halt, fall out, grab some grass, we will have a break and then trot back, well if that's alright with you, sure is we said. Murray was in his early fifties and had served in several war zones, his was experience, but I think Mc Cann's instructions came from the book.

The war in Germany is in it's last days, the Russians are in Berlin and the city has surrendered but it will be a few days before all resistance has stopped and the unconditional surrender is signed by all parties.

There have already been some shocking discoveries in the civilian concentration camps, so many dead bodies, and the way they died makes it even more necessary that the people involved in these murders be hung by the neck until dead. though this manner of death would be too quick.

At last it has come, the end of the war in Europe. The leaders have signed the documents, and Churchill has spoken to the nation, not one of his stiring speeches but a speech of genuine thanks to all people of the world that have fought to over throw "this most vile of regimes", and tomorrow is to be V E day "Victory in Europe day" the country will be on holiday to relax, after six years, we are ready, Oh so ready.

To make this most important day the commanding officer has given us permission to go outside the gate, and two of my mates in the chalet and myself are heading that way.

There by the gate is a large mirror, over the top is written ARE YOU A CREDIT TO YOUR UNIT? and if we are not we will not get passed the guy in the red hat, (Military police). We have all passed and the people of Blackpool were marvellous, we have had free Ice cream (wartime) tea and cakes in peoples houses, and free beer from guys in the pubs, the people of Blackpool literally gave us the freedom of the city, it was a fantastic day.

A fantastic day indeed, just to get out of camp to be among civillians instead of khaki city, but right now I feel a bit of a fraud.

"Alas ,concience doth make cowards of us all" I don't know who wrote those words but they seem to fit my mood tonight.

I am laying on my bunk in our chalet, my three mates sound as if they are asleep. I am thinking how I cursed my luck at being brought nearly 3oo miles to join the army here in Lancashire where the rest of the new recruits spoke a dozen different accents and not one from the South, only myself spoke "Kings English" I have today been amongst some of the people who speak with one of those accents and they were great. I felt so at home though so far from home.

That marvellous hospitality was lavished on me because I wore the uniform of the British army, an army second to none, but I had only worn that uniform a few weeks, and I would have to admit to being a reluctant soldier, just looking for excitement. I joined because the war office said I must, and to get away from spraying paint. The guys that really deserved today's show of appreciation are of course still at their posts.

I have cursed that Scots corporal Mc Cann, mainly because of his "foriegn language", but also because of the power he has over me "All power corrupts, absolute power corrupts absolutly"

As we stand on parade he bellows out his abuse we all come in for it, I feel it is designed to grind us into the dust and like the phoenix we will rise Ist class soldiers.

My problem is I think, I have never taken abuse from anyone without throwing it straight back, now I must stand and take it, and not say a word. if I did, it would be termed insolence, and I would be quickly in the guard room on a charge.

I think of some of his endearing remarks like, get your arse down it will be seen for miles, load that rifle with thumb and finger, not the palm of your hand, you will not live to pull the trigger. Move faster you are sitting ducks, you might as well consider yourselves dead right now. Mc Cann really has a way with words.

I would like to shove a nice big haggis in his big mouth, but lying here tonight I have decided that he holds the power and I might just as well accept the fact.

I have also decided that tomorrow he might just see the faintest sign of his first rate soldier, I realise now that what he is trying to teach me could be the difference between life and death.

Tomorrow when he inspects our appearance on parade and my steely blue eyes meet his murky brown eyes in our usual icy stare, he might just detect this slight change, I hope it does not spoil his day, I have even learnt a little Glaswegian.

It is the first day of peace in Europe and may it last for a thousand years, but I find it ironic when I think of all we have been through and what the aggressors actually achieved. Millions have died, often the most appalling deaths, millions have lot everything, their homes, their family, their eyes, arms, legs, even their minds, they are emotionally and financially distroyed, and those who brought these tragic conditions on these tragic people have gained nothing.

The German leader Hitler in the 1930s had a fertile plain on which to sow his seeds of hate, and it quickly grew into the fanatical nationalism that he wanted. As he thumped the desk in front of him issuing his threats, with the military bands playing and the flags waving, the people came running. The adoration spurred him on to greater threats to the world. It was like a snowball running downhill it was unstopable. as it grew and grew it carried Hitler and gang along.

The German Reich was invinceable, the i1914-1918 defeat would be avenged. Now six years later the war has only brought the German people massive distruction of their country. The cream of their young men lie in the mud of Russia, and around the world. Their women weep at home, may Germany choose peace, and compromise in the years to come, and not war.

I have rather let my mind run away with me, I have woken myself up completely with my soul searching, goodness knows what Mc Cann has in mind for us tomorrow, better get some sleep, Good night.

This is my last week of basic training, and today it is bayonet practice. Having practiced speedy fixing of the bayonet we are now in a large area of sand around which are ten dummies and we have to charge around this square and stick the bayonet into each one.

Now the sand is dry, and our big army boots sink in with each step, it is rather tough going. As we do this Mc Cann our "cheer leader" balls out his instructions, he stands well away from the dummies, good sense on his part I think. His main instruction is that we must shout, does not matter what, but it must be loud it will demoralise our enemy, louder! louder! louder! it seems we young men have great difficulty in screaming, perhaps when its for real we might do better. We have worked up quite an appetite and into the mess hall we charge, on the table are plates of bread and margarine and tins of jam, the first man grabs a handful of bread a little more than his fair share. A corporal at the table seeing this sarcastically says, not enough? have some more, so the man did, the corporal said no more, just looked as if he was glad we were the last intake.

We are off to the firing range today and sergeant Murray is in charge, as we get to the range it begins to rain, Squad Halt! put your packs on the grass and fall in on the road we then march to the guns which today are Bren guns, light machine guns about three feet long mounted on a tripod. We lie on our stomachs left hand on the butt, right hand on the trigger, line up the rear sight with the centre of the foresight and fire. I have to say my Bren shooting was awful, not at all like my rifle shooting.

We had been warned to hold it very tight, but it still danced as if that tripod was made of rubber.

Now it is to the hand grenade area, this was two brick walls about fifteen feet apart. This is a bit scarey, it involves priming our own grenade inserting the detonator, then standing there holding it until sergeant Murray calls next, and we run to where he is behind one of the walls, pull the pin, throw it and get down quick.

If all goes well there will be a loud bang on the other side, unfortunatly one man has thrown and there was no bang. Sergeant Murry looks most displeased, after a suitable time lapse it is his job to crawl out and retrieve the grenade and dump it in a hole by the side of the range. Murray gives the man the benifit of the doubt and say's it might have been the detonator.

Glad that is over, we march back to where we left our packs, we lift them up and under them the grass is dry, but we are soaked, still it would have been very difficult doing what we have wearing our capes, it is probably in the manual, how to make a hardend soldier.

Today is "THE DAY" the last day of our six weeks basic training our passing our parade. We have been checked and double checked by sergeant Murray and corporal Mc Cann, trousers with a crease you could cut your hand on, brasses gleaming in the sun, our army boots well shone, and each with the regulation twenty steel studs in each sole.

The major, his officer and the scourge of all recruits RSM Gobshite are now on the saluting platform and the CSM gives the order, Parade will advance, by the right quick march, and away we go as we pass the major the CSM gives the command, eyes right and we do as in structed. When we have all been round and done our bit, the order comes "Parade Halt", and five hundred tiny feet with whacking great army boots crash into the tarmac.

We now await the majors comments, hopefully we have measured up to that first rate soldier that the company sergeant major said he would have or else. Parade shun, you never hear the "atten" this is followed by parade stand at ease, and the major begins his routine speech that he gives when each intake is about to leave camp.

As you all know you were the last intake and I have instructed my officers and NCOs to make sure that you did not disgrace our previous record, and you did not, my congratulations.

The speech went on for some time, our six weeks training was over. The order was given to march off, by the right, quick march, and our NCO marched us back to our chalet lines, "Platoon halt" no crashing of boots on tarmac this time as our chalet lines are on sand.

Sergeant Murray is a man of few words, he say's we have been a good bunch and wishes ue all the best, Corporal Mc Cann is not a man of few words.

I have to say you have done well, but sergeant Murray and myself have had to work dammed hard to get it out of you. You came here and left behind all those comforts that Mummy lavished on you, and what replaced it was somewhat different. it was our job to turn boys into soldiers, fit for battle, trained to stay alive, dead soldiers are not good to the army.

You were the last intake ,there have been many through this camp, I have learned quickly to recognise those that would slit my throat and think nothing of it, and it seemed his gaze lingered on me for a moment but we always come to understand each other (slight laugh)

Well I wish you all the best of luck, keep your heads down, remember all you have been taught, and stay alive.

Sergeant Murray and I have done our bit, tomorrow you will parade as normal, but you will be under "admin" who will tell you what units you will now join and where you will go. That is it then, if you see me in the NAAFI tonight you can all buy me a pint (another polite laugh) and squad dismiss, HOO-RAY.

The NAAFI is our sort of club where we can have a drink and get some food to supplement our rather meagre diet. We shall all be there tonight being as it is our last night here and it is going to be one to remember, but first I must visit the neighbouring platoon. While on parade today I heard a sergeant discussing a few last minute details with his corporal, the sergeant was obviously Welsh, but the corporal was unmistakenly a Londoner. I have been in this camp for six weeks and did not know there was another "English speaking" man here, I have just got to meet him. The lads tell me where he is, I bang on the chalet door, and when he opens it I say "watch ere mate" and he looks absolutly astounded, and then seeing the beaming grin on my face bursts out laughing.

Crikey mate are you from the "smoke" (London) ,No I said but close, down in Kent. We had a darn good natter, you would have thought we were meeting in darkest Africa.

What is your name? he asked, just call me Huck, I said, O K I'm Charlie see you in the Naafi tonight? sure will, I'll buy you a pint, I'll be there, we shook hands again and could not help laughing it was great to hear a southern voice.

One thing does worry me a bit ,before going on parade this morning Jock says "ere is this your pay book"? I felt where it should have been and obviously the one on the floor was mine. The problem was that before handing it too me he had looked inside, ere he said is that what Huck is short for Huckleberry? I had to say yes, he had a dammed good laugh,, then said sorry and laughed again.

Since coming here I have always been "private" Hawn on parade and Huck when not on parade, now Jock knows, how long before everyone knows I wondered. I decided I would try a damage limitation exercise and said, I would appreciate it Jock if this could be just between we two, Ah ya do na need to worry Mac ya secret is safe with me. Thanks mate I said, but I knew it would not be wise to bet on it, the secret of being a good soldier is to raise a laugh. No point in worrying about that, tonight is our last night and they will hear us down in Kent.

We have grouped several tables together and are all around them, on the tables are a variety of bottles, my new friend has invited his fellow ScotJock and his fellow Scot Mc Cann to join us, Mc Cann will not pass up a free drink.

Corporals must use the Naafi like us, but sergeants have their own sergeants mess, it will be very interesting to see if Mc Cann will let his hair down and be one of us tonight. It was noticable how he rolled up when all the beer was on the table, perhaps I am being a little unfair on Jocks fellow Scot.

After a few pints and a bit of friendly abuse of Scots, and Londoners, our chalet Scot Jock suggested a song, good idea who will sing it? How about the guy with the longest name said Jock. Who is that? came the chorus, well Huck he said, that's not long said John, it is when you take the whole name Is'nt it Huck, a loud cheer got me off the hook and I stood up. What is it to be? how about Lilly Marlene, that would be great said my Scots friend. Standing up was not good enough, two guys who don't stand too well themselves heave me up on a chair, the beer has removed, all inhibitions I might have had, and away we go.

The song Lilly Marlene was German, but it was sung as much by the British soldier as the German. It told of a soldier confined to camp who knows his girl friend is waiting on the other side of the gates, "I knew you were waiting in the street, I heard your feet but could not meet, my Lilly on the lamplight, my own Lilly Marlene." What kind of job I made of it was difficult to say, as the whole Naafi joined in, and there was a rousing cheer at the end not for me, but because they had enjoyed the singing it with me, and because we were celebrating.

O K now what about a song from the Scots? yeah how about it? only if we have one from the Londoners said the Scot, no bovver, said corporal Charlie and me.

It was of course obvious what the two Jock's would sing. "I belong to Glasgow, dear old Glasgow town" we all knew it, where ever there were Scots you would hear that song, but it was good to see a smile on Mc Cann's face, although it might have been just our beer.

Of course as the evening went on the beer on the table grew less, and the group were a little less clear in their speech, there was just the chance that our Scots might have forgotten the Londoners contribution. No chance, Mc Cann with a little difficulty getting his words right say's "I've nay forgotten laddies ye were going to sing a song were ye not? What is it to be? lets be hearing form ya" there was just a hint of the corporal there, but no matter. I was not a Londoner of course but to a Scot I sounded the same.

Corporal Charlie and me sang that old Flanigan and Allen song, Underneath the Arches, that was about as "London" as you would get. "Underneath the Arches we dream our dreams away, sorry when the day light comes streaming ,heralding the dawn"

The song meant a lot to us, but most guys were a little worse for ware, not much applause this time, "dreams" seems to be in the minds of some of the lads round the table. Some now have their Arms and heads on the table. We are all a bit that way, it does not matter about us, we don't have far to go to our chalet, but the two corporals must not be seen in their state at the moment.

I have certainly not had much time for Mc Cann, but tonight he has been o k and has entered into the spirit of our celebration so I would not want to see him or corporal Charlie on a charge'.

It will soon be lights out and so we wake our sleeping drinkers and having got them on their feet we head for the door, and as we go through we see the two corporals having a chat, the words were a little slured but they understood them.

It has been a great end to our life at Squires Gate training camp, and I shake hands with my fellow Londoner, corporal Charlie and say, I hope to se you before I go tomorrow, and to my astonishment Mc Cann puts his hand out, and we shake hands, and with a grin he say's, It has nay been so bad has it Laddie? no it's nay been so bad I said.

We drift back to our chalets happy to think that the toilets are not far away. Jock is up on his bunk he chose the top one as a at six feet three inches it is easier for him to get up there than it would be for the rest of us. He raises an imaginary glass. To my new friends in chalet No 5, and we all cheer, and I return it. to our good friend Jock, just wish I could understand him, he makes an effort to get down from his bunk but thinks better of it, I'm pleased about that. All is quiet but as Jock rolls over he has the last word, blethering sasanachs, his term for the English.

Our last day here has been a fitting end to our six weeks training together, "should auld aquiantance be forgot" I doubt it.

We are a little reluctant to get out of bed this morning, but we don't linger long, the CSM does not accept excuses. It was a great evening and we have the heads to prove it.

We have now done the usuals, and now we are on parade with the CSM giving the orders. Parade Attention, stand at ease, and then he tells us what will happen to us all today.

You will observe positions around the parade ground, each with three letters of the alphabet, you will on my dismissing the parade go to one of these positions. You will on your own name being called march smartly up, give your name and number and you will be told where to go next, what regiment you will join.
Transport will be here precisely at eleven hundred hours to take you and your kit to the station. In the mean time you will take your bedding to the stores, see all your kit is in your kit bag and see the chalet is clean, is that clear? SIR.
From CSM upwards such a lecture and question is answered by a loud "sir". SIR dismisses the parade and I march smartly up to the table with the officer behind it. When I get to the table I stamp my boots hard on the tarmac, throw up a beautiful salute and shout out 24969276 private Hawn Sir.

Right Hawn I hope you have enjoyed your say here, now it is time to move on, here are your papers for your next unit, and your railway warrent to get you there, Good luck. I take the papers, take one step back, another heavy stamp of boots, throw up another beauty, right turn, and that's my lot I am on my way.

When I looked at those papers I nearly let out a loud ya hoo, I have been posted to RASC Southend. I'm going back south, I am over the moon, but I could not help smiling ,they drag one man from Kent to Lancashire, and after six weeks training they send him back, still I'm certainly not complaining.

I've nipped along to see my London mate corporal Charlie, we will keep in touch, now it is up in the truck and away we go, through that gate for the last time and we are well and truly on our way when we let out an ear shattering cheer,, but that sour faced M.P could not even raise a grin, every soldier hated the military police. My three chalet mates are staying in the North so I am on my own going South.

In my compartment is a clergyman, an old lady with her two grand children, a guy about thirty, over in the corner, and right opposite is a soldier with dark glasses. He has a hat that makes me think he is an Australian. I am not sure but I think he is looking quite hard at me, then he say's, been in long? no I said I've just done my six weeks basic training. He laughed, I remember that, glad that's over aint you mate, sure am I said.

You look as if you have service I said, yes he said I sailed from Sydney, joined Montgomery at El Alamein, beat the Grrmans, The Afrika Korp, did the Sicilly job, into Italy, and that is where I lost my eye, so my fighting days were over.

That was dammed tough luck mate, could have been worse, much worse he said. I was flown back to the U K, had my operation in a famous eye hospital, but I left behind in Italy thousands of Germans, they all have both eyes, but are all dead. I buried some of them myself so I figure I got the best deal. So it ain't so bad mate, I am alive those bastards are dead, well here's my stop he put his hand out, I said thanks for coming, he laughed and said, well I can't say it was a pleasure, still keep your head down see you in Sydney, and he was gone.

The young boy was full of thought about the Aussie soldier as was his Grandma, but I wondered what the guy in the corner felt.

It reminded of the guy that asked my brother Bill why he was not in the army and Bill floored him. I suppose it is just possible that he might be unfit for service, anyway it's over now, or nearly. Well I think that is the end of any interesting conversation, the churchman has still go this head in his book, the guy in the corner is still looking out of the window, and the elderly lady is looking at me as if she wondered if I would end up the same way as the Aussie, so I think I will have a snooze, the train must stop when it gets to London.

The screech of brakes, the loud speaker system, and the noise from the platform tell me I am in London. That to me was a marvellous feeling. I have a little time to kill so I make my way to the church army canteen for a mug of tea and a bun. They and other organisations like the salvation army were great, and I don't think I ever saw one of these ladies without a smile.

I have arrived at Southend, now out of the station and a guy in a jeep gives me a lift to my new address. When I arrive at the RASC camp it is almost dark, and when I report to the guardroom the guard commander say's, your a bit late aren't you, and I point out that I had come all the way from Blackpool, Oh yes, so you have.

Well if you nip over to the cookhouse you might still be in time for some supper, then you had better kip in the games room and we will run you up to your billet tomorrow. I got my mug of tea and a sandwich after a little pleading, they too reminded me that I was late.

The games room had just a table tennis table, and a billard table, not wishing to sleep on the floor I slipped my boots off made myself a pillow, and that was going to be my bed. It had a cover on it, and I was dog tired so I managed to sleep but that was the hardest bed I have ever had.

In the morning the duty driver ran me up to what was to be my next army hotel. This really was a hotel it had two conical towers, large bay windows and was called the Palmiara Towers Hotel. Your not having me on are you mate? I said, no, come on in and in we went, the rooms were quite large with four beds, that's Jims, over in that corner is Steve, this is mine, and that's yours blimey a little different from Squires gate, I seem to have had the army all wrong.

Blackpool, Southend, hotel accomdation I think I might just get used to this.

Better be going Huck I have got to take you to workshops. The Royal Army Service Corp is a transport regiment with work shops to service the vehicles.
Back at Squires gate we had been asked which branch of the army we would rather join, and looking for a cushy number not wishing to become a brigadier, I said I would like to continue in my trade.

Now electricians become cooks, and cooks become electricians in the army, but I never for one moment thought that this coach painter would become a coach painter. I reported to the workshops officer who quickly gave me to the work shops sergeant who having introduced me to the other tradesman gave me a trade test.
This was some what degrading, they gave me a large truck canopy which I spread out on thr road, they then gave me a gallon of paint and a four inch brush and said "paint it" Needless to say I passed the test, and my pay book now reads coach painter grade three, and I am intitled to the magniticent sum of one pound fifty pence a week.

I am glad to have left the bull shine behind and be back repairing trucks, not much has changed just that these are army trucks, back in Ashford they were Air Ministry trucks. Being a tradesman does not get me out of all the bull shine, we still do guard duty and this is where I nearly dropped into the proverial.

While the guard was being inspected my mate whispers a funny I grinned and the guard commander saw me, what are you grinning at nothing sergeant, do you always grin at nothing? occasionally, I said you should see a psychiatrist, he said I've seen one, I knew by now I was in deep trouble and the next move was the sergeants.
Right Hawn we will continue this conversation in the morning, at least I had all night to think of a way out, but by morning I still have not come up with anything. Fortunately at guard dismounting next morning no reference was made of our conversation of the previous evening much to my relief.

After that Southend was great, pity the Kersal Pleasure gardens were still closed, but the town was trying to get back to its 1939 image.

Because the war in Europe is over we were apt to forget that the guys in the far East are still fighting. An American aircraft carrier has been attacked by the Japanese suicide pilots who fly their planes and bombs straight at the target. The carrier The Bunker Hill was turned into a fireball and 400 men died amazingly the ship did not sink. The Japanese know their days are numbered, their troops are being winkled out from their holes by the Americans, and the Aussies, it cannot be long now.

August the sixth and a terrible act of war has taken place thousands of Japanese have been incinerated by the first Atomic Bomb, and the city of Hiroshima almost completly distroyed, any survivors have had a massive dose of radiation and we in the free world who have known what Japanese cruelty can be, feel no pity for them what so ever, this is retribution for the suffering they have caused to so many countries, especially China.

The first Atomic bomb has been used, even now faced with such awful suffering of its people they still would not accept that they were defeated, and so another Japanese city and its people had to suffer the same fate. Three days later Nagasaki was the target for atomic bomb number two, thousands more were burnt where they stood, this time there was no alternative and on Sunday September 2nd almost six years since we were forced to go to war the Japanese surrendered.

General Mac Arthur who was forced to evacuate an Island by the Japanese now had the enormous satisfaction of receiving their surrender. He chose to do this on the American battleship Missourie anchored in the bay of the Japanese capitol Tokyo. How sweet is revenge when one thinks of all the men who have died fighting the Japs, and how bitter the taste of defeat, when there is no way to save face.

So now it is all over and for what!
For the Japanese, German's and Italian's, death distruction, and defeat, for the free world, freedom. Freedom for each nation to live as it's people desire, without domination by a foreign army, or fannatical politions, but at what a cost, Oh what a price was paid, and those who will never come back, can never be repaid.

Rest in peace old comrades, rest in peace. At the going down of the sun, and in the morning, we will remember you. That is what we will be doing here in Aldershot today.

Huckleberry Hawn

I have moved on again I am now in Aldershot, the home of the British Army, I guess it was too good to last, Blackpool, Southend, it was looking really good, but all good things come to an end.

Aldershot *is* the army, if you picked a wide road with a good surface, plenty of street lights etc., chances are you would just find yourself in another regimental area.

Today we have marched to this large parade ground, the area is full, and outside on the approach roads there are many more. two to three thousand men from a number of regiments. We are about to march through; the town to celebrate the end of the war and to mark VJ day, victory over Japan.
Many of those lining the route will have lost a member of their family and as we march by victorious, they may feel that he or she did not die in vain.

We have almost a mile to march before we enter the town centre The units on the road are now moving off, when we get the order we on the parade ground will move out onto the road, and already the leading unit is almost out of sight. It is a most impressive turnout.

Although I am a soldier of only four months, I am already feeling a sense of great pride. A lot of those guys have fought for five or six years and this is what they fought for.

We are all on the road now mainly Khaki, some Navy Blue, the red berets of the Airborn divisions, and just in front of us are the Scots, with all the colour of a Scots regiment.

This is great as I love pipe music and these guys have played them all over the world in many battle areas, and to a Scot (and me) the pipes and drums really put fire in the belly. Spaced out along this great parade are four other bands, fortunatly far enough a part because of the lenghh of the parade, but what a feeling, thousands of army boots crashing onto the road, military music, the beat of the drums, and the cheering waving people shouting their greetings, this is indeed another day I will not forget. We have passed through the town like true victors and made our way to the dispersal area where we shall be addressed by the Brigadier. He has impressed on us the main reason for this parade, but more importantly to remember the men and women who will not be coming home. After his congratulations on the parade ,we are dismissed and the rest of day is ours, V J Day.

Being a new boy here I have been asked by four of the old soldiers if I would like to join them down town, and of course I was very happy to accecpt, not much to do in the afternoon but in the evening there were the pubs, and because of its large soldier content there were plenty of them.
These guys are old soldiers they have done this all around the world, and I was a raw recruit and so was not surprised by what happened next.
Alex and leader of the pack ,very well liked by the men and the ATS (women's army), say's to the bar maid, six pints of bitter please, this of course was a little strange as there was only five of us. There are the six pints lined up on the bar and Alex say's now, Huck is going to down this pint in one go ,if he does not he will pay for the whole lot, O K Huck‖

Well having always had a great respect for money I decided that it just had to be done, but I was sure glad to see the bottom of the glass. I received a cheer for my efforts, Alex handed me the spare pint and we made our way to a table. Before the evening was over I realised that this little group of squaddies had done this many times, and that their capacity was some what greater than mine, but we obviously got back to camp alright as I woke up in my own bunk.

V J day was indeed a great day, a fitting end to six years of war and a day when we were all justifiably proud.

Today I am on my way to REME workshops Ashford courtesy of my workshops Captain. When I first arrived here I reported to company office, and to the officer commanding, after the usual details the Captain asked ,where do you come from Hawn? Ashford Kent Sir, Great Scot that is where I come from, I am Captain Geering, you know our shop in the High Street don't you? yes of course Sir I said, sensing I was on a winner here.

He would I think liked to carry on chatting but it would not have been proper, as officers and private's do not mix. Tell you what Hawn, we often have a truck going to REME Ashford, next time they go I will get you on it, Thank you Sir I said with a beautiful salute, a little boot licking could pay dividends. I had several trips but sadly Captain Geering moved on.

The guys I worked with were mostly old soldiers waiting for demob, to get back to civilian life, but they were a good laugh especially when the A T S Girls come to collect their vehicles, Alex was always the charmer he had them eating out of his hand. In general I found Aldershot rather boring and was glad to move on.

I am now at Botley, a village about five miles outside Southampton, it is another mixed camp, RASC transport and work shops, and the A T S girls do all the driving. I like it here, it is quite an easy going place, long wooden huts with a couple of tortoise stoves and the usual bunk beds. I am glad to have one of the bottom ones.

One of the snags for a new boy is that the old soldiers from the battle areas are coming home and are keen to have a laugh at my expense, but that is O K by me.

One of the duties we have to do is telephone duty, which involves sleeping in the office. I am in the office doing my "duty" when there is a knock at the door and in walks Nancy.

Nancy is a slim good looking gal, with a beaming smile and some thing under her arm, and as she worked in the office I thought nothing of it.

She sits down on the bed that I am sitting on and starts drawing, after a while she hands me the finished drawing and asks me what I thought, I said it was very good and full of detail. It was a drawing of a girl with nothing on ,she draws another with the same request, for my opinion, and as I said, the drawing did not lack detail! I am by now considering my next course of action, Nancy is pushing her luck, however the art class was brought to an untimely end when Enid, Nancy's office mate walks in.

It might have been just as well because I found out next day that the lads had suggested it to Nancy to see what would happen, but unfortunatly for them they never told Enid, so although we all had a good laugh it was not all on me.

I had a laugh a couple of weeks ago, well more of a quiet grin I had just got back off leave, it was almost 11-49 p m everyone asleep or so I thought, just got into my bunk when there was a tapping at the window, and again tap, tap, tap I thought we had ghosts like "Wuthering Heights", but it all became clear when the guy opposite got out of his bunk, and went out of the door, and through the window, in the moonlight I saw the "Ghost", she was tall and quite well built, I never heard him come back.

I definitly like it here, the huts are good, the food is great and it is served up by some very good humoured A T S girls but I guess I won't be here long Southend and Aldershot were rather short stays. Being only five miles from Southampton it is great to go and see the big liners come in, and with a bit of cheek I get down on the quay, the uniform helps a lot.

It is getting near to christmas now and the whole workshops seem to be making kids toys, it sure is a good camp. Most guys would like to go home for christmas but we cannot all go and I am one of those who will be here for the festivities, but being an easy going camp it will not be so bad.

Christmas day and the customary Turkey is being served with of course, stuffing, this is ideal for the camp clown Private Grimmet. He is in the queue for his dinner, he waits until he is about to get his. Then he turns to the queue and bawles out, who wants stuffing? of course he gets a good laugh. This guy has plenty of cheek, he rides his cycle out of the main gate with a ladder on his shoulder and a can of paint on his handle bars, and goes painting in the village. Nobody says a word, a very easy going camp.

I came here in October and as I expected am on the move again this time it is overseas, where, we will not be told. To prepare for this we are in South Wales where we will be kitted out for our intended destination. I have been here three days and it has rained almost all the time, the whole area is mud and duck boards, I shall not be returning to Wales.

We have been given a new uniform, very thin material "Khaki Drill" this is for hot climates and the hot climate connot come soon enough.

Hooray, we are leaving this swamp and heading for Newhaven where we will board a ferry for Dieppe, and then a train across France to Toulon. Mid channel now and the white cliffs have almost disappeared, the sea is rough, and I am also feeling a bit rough. I've been up on deck and now I am below deck, but think I will go back on deck near the rail. I did not think much of the sea trip, and I am not optimistic about the long train ride.

We are now on the train, it is cold, the seats are just wooden seats, the only consolation is that we have been given a blanket It is so cold, and with the blanket wrapped around me I give it one more tug, and that last tug has done something to my stomach and it is painful, but there are no medics, I will have to wait until we are on board ship.

Toulon and the Mediterranean and in the harbour is our boat. It is quite a big one so I hope it won't bounce around like the ferry. One day out and feeling sick with a very painful stomach, I am going to the sick bay to see the Doc. My appearance at the medical bay has caused a bit of a problem it seems, they have to put out a call over the ships loud speeker system to call the doctor out.

I do not feel too popular! The doctor arrives dressed for dinner obviously not at all pleased to see me, my pain alnost disappears. Well what's your problem? not much sign of bedside manner, I explained what happened, get up on there, and I heave myself up on the slab, raise yourself up, lower, up again, right you have pulled a stomach muscle, it was a rapid diagnosis. I suppose, but dammed painful.

I thought, a bit of medication and I'll be on my way, but no, he was getting interested. He called his medical orderlies in, right he say's this chap has pulled a stomach muscle, observe, raise yourself up man, down, up again and down, see that? see where it trouble him most, I knew where it troubled him most, even if they did not. Give him a wide support bandage and some pain killer and I will see you in three days, and with that he was gone.

Is he always that abrupt I said to the orderly or has he got something spoiling? he is always like that, but tonight he may well have something spoiling.

That bandage helped alot but getting up into a ships hammock to sleep was hell, fortunatly there was a big buy next to me and he helped to heave me up into it, the trick was not to fall out the other side.

Being January the Mediterranean sun is not that hot but the water is clear and blue, well it was, but the cooks have just throw the swill over the side, still it made a bit of entertainment. The Dolphins that always seem to be with us either astern, or along side are having a great time, a joy to watch.

On the Horizon is the Egyption coast, in about five hours we shall be in Port Said harbour.

I shall be very glad to leave the ship, I have not been sick just felt like it, but most of all I shall be glad to leave behind that perishing hammock, they are normally very comfortable but not if you have a stomach muscle problem.

In harbour another piece of entertainment, there are Arab boats along side us trying to sell us their goods, the method being to lower a rope and basket ,the Arab puts the good sin the basket, and the customer sends down the money, well most times.

Off the ship now and on the train not very comfortable just wooden seats and bags of fresh air, but a little more entertainment. It seems some Arabs have been stealing from the people on the train. There now come two Arabs running through the carriage, followed by two policemen, the thieving Arabs run into the arms of more police who carry sticks like cricket stumps. The two Arabs are beaten by the police cricket stumps and thrown off the train, which is doing about thirty miles an hour, quite effective I thought, and a marked saving on Lawyers fees.

Our journey comes to an end at a large camp called a "holding area" here men and materials are sent to all camps over a large area.

My number has come up and my destination is El Kirsh and to get there I have to travel on the train on my own, and with a load of Arabs, I don't feel too comfortable. I get out at my station and report to the R T O (Railway transport officer) who aranges transport to the camp at El Kirsh.

While waiting I see trucks coming into the yard with 71 on their vehicles and having got fed up with waiting I said to one of those guys have you seen any 44 company trucks? we are 44 company he said, and I said, well why the hell do you have 71 on the truck, don't know mate, hop in. and I was sure glad to do just that. I was pleased to be on the truck heading for what I hoped would be some kind of civilisation but quickly realised I was heading away from it. It was a reasonable road but all around for as far as the eye could see was sand, nothing but dirty greyish sand, and when we came to the camp at El Kirsh I had that same feeling I had on my first day at Squires Gates, just the sand was a different colour.

I report to company office and I am directed to workshops and tent areas, even the workshops were tubular frames and canopy my vision of harems, and arabian nights has definitly gone.

My first tea break was a bit of a laugh ,as we sat on our large boxes, large beetles were running through the sand, that is one of ours said one of the old soldiers, what do you mean I asked || well look, he has our red spot on his back, maybe they have been out here too long!.

They certainly were very keen to get home, a lot of them had fought in Italy, and were due to go home, but until more guys like me come out from the U K they cannot go home, and this makes them very re-luctant soldiers, as I found out a few days ago.

This night was my first guard duty, we have been given our positions and mine was to patrol the wire perimeter, it is almost dark and the wild dogs are howling like wolves, a little scarey to say the least. The guy I walk out of the door with is a real old soldier, and as I set off on my patrol he say's hey where are you going? round the wire I said. You don't want to do that ,hop up in this cab and have a kip, well it did not seem quite right, but I did not need a lot of persuading, and we did just that. We fell asleep and when I woke it was half an hour after we should have been relieved.

Now we were in trouble, no soldier if he is doing his job properly would ever miss the guy who comes out to take over the position, we have got a bit of a problem here mate so you had best let me do the talking, you just nod in the right places, this I was more than ready to do.

My fellow guardsman was a guy called Weaver, he was a Yorkshire man, a good soldier I am sure, but his demob number has come and gone and if replacements had come from the U K he would now be at home. These guys have done their bit and they are getting restless.

I have no idea what is about to take place but as a new boy I am not looking forward to it. Here is the guard room and in we go. Where the hell have you two been? we've been looking all a over for you. Well you did'nt look hard enough did you. We have done an extra half hour ,we could have been in our bunks, I don't suppose you will knock half hour off our next shift? no I dammed well will not! I am going to forget it for tonight, but if it happens again on my guard you will be on the fizzer, got it? get your tea! The guard commander did not ask me any questions he did not have to, he knew Weavers story was a load of bull, but he also knew that the feeling in the camp was a little explosive.

No trouble with our next shift, four till six, we make our way back to the guard room, it is almost 6 a m and the sun has risen, and the guard is dismissed and I am relieved i more ways than one. We have done two shifts of two hours, and a bit of sleep in between, and now I am at work.

I have to respray an officers car, I have it all ready when he comes to see me, and it's quite funny, the paint I have to use is a dull grey sandy colour without a trace of gloss. I want it to shine painter he say's, sorry sir can't do that, why ever not he say's, I have no varnish or linseed oil to put into the paint, well use engine oil man! I am afraid that will not do sir I said respectfully, of course it will man! do it! Well I knew what would happen and so I was quite liberal with the engine oil and on it went. With the heat of the sun it dried with a brilliant shine, but within a month most of it was peeling off. That guy was a pain in the proverbial, a real text book officer, the kind of man the men despise, and fellow officers avoid.

What did annoy me was having to respray it and re write all the signs on it, all vehicles had to have English registration plate, Arabic plate, four divisional signs, tyre pressures all round, and a large white star on the bonnet, still although I could not say it, he knew what I was thinking, I told you so! little Hitlers do annoy me.

Guards come round every three days and we have had a few moans about it, any way I am on again tonight, and this time my position is the petrol dump. This is an area almost as big as a football pitch, it is stacked with thirty five gallon drums of petrol and I am supposed to patrol the area. I don't like the idea of that, the area is on rocks and my big army boots would tell anyone just where I was, and so I find myself a spot out of the light of the perimeter light, and just listen, and so the element of surprise is with me, not them.

There are a lot of guys round here who really do deserve the title "thieving swines" This guard post is a very noisy one as all these drums of petrol would have expanded with the heat of the sun during the day and would contract with the cold night with a loud boom. This loud boom coupled with the howling wild dogs, like the wolves of the "Yucon" makes the end of the shift very welcome, the only snag is, you know in four hours time you will be back there.

It seems we have been allowing the workshops to become untidy ,and we have allowed oil to build up on yhe concrete so the commanding officer has decreed that we clean it, in our own time. On Saturday afternoons we would probably be under our mosquito nets on our bunks, writing home, but this afternoon it is the big clean up. It's not being here so much that annoys me it is the guy in charge, Staff sergeant Moots a useless individual of about twenty three years. He has told a couple of guys to bring a thirty five gallon drum of petrol over and is now telling them to pour it over the yard, this, while a man is welding at the other end of the yard. This has infuriated by guard mate Weaver who has launched into a torrent of abuse of this NCO. Of all the stupid things to do ,petrol and welding torches, you are pathetic a ruddy disgrace, you are putting mens lives in danger and you have not got the sense to see it. Well you are not risking mine, if you want me I'll be on my truck and away he went.

The sergeant was as Weaver said pathetic. He should put Weaver on a charge for insubordination, but he did not say a word just carried on directing the flow of petrol with a stupid grin on his face, like a boy who has just pinched his friends marbles. Weaver was a good guy he just had a little difficulty with idiots, he was a Yorkshire man who called a spade a spade.

Today he is a happy man, ten replacements have arrived and he is going home. Well earned, and long overdue. He has been a popular driver and is now going round the workshops saying his farewells, and now he is with me. Hello Huck I'm on my way at last, yes I said, I wish I was going with you, and he laughed, if he had his way we would all be going home.

Sorry about that guard duty Huck, I should not have suggested you did not do your job, I set a bad example, no bother mate I said, you talked us both out of it, and we both laughed. We shook hands and with a grin off he went. He climed up in the truck and after a bit of banter the truck moved off, and as it passed company office a Yorkshire voice rang out "don't forget lads never let the baskets see they have got you". We will miss old Weaver.

The replacements have been a bit of a problem they have had three engine fires in their trucks, the other drivers used a petrol rag to clean their engines with no bother but the new boys have also been using wire brushes and have produced sparks.

Today I have had a marvellous surprise, I saw two RAF men go into the office and they are now heading my way, not wishing to get involved I carried on writing the signs on the truck. They stopped and the workshops officer say's, Hawn, do you know this man I turned, and laughed, yes Sir he is my brother Les.

The captain left us, and there was so much to talk about. He told me he was at RAF Moascer, about two miles from Ishmalia, and if I could get on the weekend truck from El Kirsh he would meet it and take me back to his RAF base. It all went according to plan and I enjoyed being in his nice conditions, what a difference, his living quarters were to my tent on the sand. He fed me well and gave me a few bits which would make life a little easier at El Kirsh.

The RAF base was like another world. Time to go now another big hand shake, see you next week? you sure will unless I am caught for duty and off I go.

I walk back into Ishmalia, through the French quarter with its green grass and sprinklers, on through the corrugated iron shacks of the very poor Egyptians and to the pick up point where the truck is waiting.

On our way back to El Kirsh we run parallel with the "Sweet Water Canal" which we are told should we get into it we will require a dozen injections, including cholera, a big one. As we go along the road a crowd of people have assembled, looking down in to the canal we see the reason, an upturned army truck. It had obviously mistook the wide area of steps leading down to the canal for a road and summersaulted into the canal. We made our way down the steps to the canal and in the water were three soldiers floating on their backs calling out "HELP", and each help seemed weaker than the previous one. I could not swim but I thought surely some of these people can. Will these RAF and Army men let these soldiers drown for the fear of a few injections.

Fortunately it did not come to that, down the steps came an RAF flight sergeant, he took his tunic off and dived in with no hesitation, and had them all out in minutes, he received a great cheer but he must have thought what a despicable bunch the rest of us were.

I have been to see Les several times but this looks like being the last one, as next week we are moving up into Palastine. We have come into Ismalia for the afternoon, and it is quite a nice town away from the corrugated iron shacks, this area where we are now is beautifully green, watered daily from the canal. Green in Egypt is really beautiful, and a photographer has approached us, we would normally tell him in Arabic where to go, but this situation of two brothers in the RAF and Army meeting in the Middle East is worth a few "piasters", glad we did it, is a great memento.

I shall miss Les quite a lot but we are on our way, the whole camp on trucks, funny thing, my shooting with the Bren machine gun was awful, but I always seem to get it. I am up in the back of the last truck with the Bren, still, with a box of magazines I am bound to hit something.

It is good to be leaving Egypt behind, too much sand and too many flies, as we pass through the border post there are Egyptian police and Palastinian police, the latter are of course British, as Palastine is a British responsibility. As we move further in the land becomes greener, there are crops in the fields, orange and eucalyptus groves, the people are maimly in white instead of black, the Jews are of course in European dress.

We have arrived and it looks great, we are still going to be in tents but at last they have concrete bases and it is a redish soil around them, not dirty grey sand. It is all systems go now if we want somewhere to sleep tonight, but putting up a twenty foot square tent to house six beds if you have never done it before is a bit of a problem.

The sergeant major tells us how to do it but it does not seem to go quite like he said, some of the other guys must have been boy scouts, theirs are almost up, well ours is up just hope we don't get a gale. The camp is now almost operational and one of the things that is most important is the company orders board. Every man needs to look at this each day to see if his name is on it, it would be no good saying sorry sir, I did not see it, no excuses accepted.

Today my name is on the board I am one of a number of men for F.F.I. this is a medical inspection to see if I am hiding any nasty disease. We are all in the sick bay and the M.O. walks in we stand, he says sit down, and we are ready.

Before I commence my examinations I am going to repeat what clearly needs repeating, judging by the number of men reporting sick with a particular problem. Since you have been here in the Middle East you will probably have noticed a number of ladies wishing to make your acquaintance, this is not because you have suddenly become irresistible to them. it is because you have money and they want some of it.

Most of these ladies have a sign outside their house which say's "OUT OF BOUNDS" quite a large sign you cannot miss it! Now if you should make contact with one of these ladies, and as it were, come face to face with her, it is virtually certain that you will be coming to see me, as part of you will be extremly painful. Should you do so you will incur my extreme dis pleasure and my sick report will go straight to the commanding officer, who will promptly place you on a charge which you will answer when you return from the hospital dealing with this particular problem. These out of bounds signs are there for your protection and to save me work, any questions?. Yes sir, how will we know if we have this problem? you will know, Oh yes you will know, it is like urinating broken glass.

Right now strip off and come in when your name is called. I have been done and my pay book has been stamped with the date and "free from infection "F.F.I.

The workshops are now operational and my rather primitive paint shop is now ready for work. Of course guards come around quite frequently, and I am on guard tonight.

Guard duty is a little different here, the country is different and the noises are not the same, apart from the wild dogs howling, with this the Arab sheperd who plays his tin whistle half the night, the water pump in the orange groves, and a few more. In a way these noises in the middle of the night are better than dead quiet, they even seem like a bit of company. Tonight I am on roving guard, I patrol the perimeter wire from post to post. I much prefer this one to standing in one position, it is a cloudy December night and while not as cold as England it is still darned cold, even with battle dress and overcoat.

As I approach the first guard post I quietly call out all right Ron? Yeah, apart from that idiot with his flute. Has the orderly officer been round yet? have not seen him, what's the time? is that all, gor blimey, Well I had better see if Fred has shot anybody yet, see you Ron. I make my way along the wire listening for every sound, as I approach Fred's post I can hear he has company, hundreds of Bull Frogs croaking in the marshy bit down by the road.

Halt! who goes there? Fred calls out too loudly, Cleopatra I say, Go on he say's come on in I need something to warm me up. All quiet Fred? yeah apart from those perishing Bull Frogs they never stop do they, if there were any thieving baskets round here I would never know, seen the orderly officer? not yet, he is probably still getting Brahms and Liszt in the officers mess, who is on tonight? Rimtol he is always hissed. One more post and I can make my way back. I need to be a bit careful with this one he is one of the new boys and it can be a bit frightening on guard on your own, in the middle of the night. I make a little more noise as I approach and call out, all right Jeff? yeah o k Huck what's the time? is that all? seems extra long tonight, only another half hour I said, Hoo blooming ray, Jeff replied. How long have you been out here Huck? nearly a year now, do you still feel a bit scared? course I do, we all do and those guys that say they don't are bull shining you, well see you later Jeff, and I make my way back along the wire.

When I get back to Fred there is no sign of him, I get right into his sandbag emplacement, when he finally shows up, ere, you been kipping? no I was not kipping, I was having a ruddy piddle O K.

Here, someone is coming Fred, you had better challenge him, yes he said, Halt! who goes there? after what seemed a lifetime, a rather slurred "Captain Rimtol" came back, advance sir said Fred, every thing all right guard? yes sir no problems, good show, now remember guard we have to be a little more careful now things are becoming a little more tense, yes sir, I'll be getting along now good night and he stumbled off down the path, that was a bit of luck Fred, he might have caught you having a piddle, Ah shove off said Fred and I made my way back to Ron.

A chat with Ron and our shift was over. We make our way back to the guard room and dip our mugs in the tea urn, drink it, and lay down on the bunk, in four hours time we will be back out there.

I did not mind that guard so much as it meant that I would not be on again until after christmas day, which is tomorrow. Christmas here starts with the duty officer and the C S M bringing us a mug of tea, and a shot of rum, if we want it, (no I kid you not) that is the custom, and it is great to have our situation reversed, they do not look too pleased, but we are.

After a lazy morning with tea and cakes in the naafi it is over to the mess hall for dinner. Right up through the hall are lines of tables with the usual things, plus a bottle of gold star beer for each man. Gold star beer is not too bad but of course it has never seen a ny Kentish hops. Our dinner is brought to us by the officers and sergeants, again it is the custom and it is great, but to give them their due they even managed a laugh.

I guess there is a time for discipline, and a time just to be men. Any spare bottles are smuggled out to continue the celebration this afternoon, the usual card school is formed and we have a few laughs, just one thing we are not sure now is how we should react over. During the afternoon Bill holds up his bottle, "The King" he say's and Smithy from under his mosquito net say's after you with The King, he known for his republican tendencies.

Over to the naafi in the evening for more of the same, but a slight difference tonight, the camp Padre has appeared, a man of the church always has an effect on ones behaviour.

Good evening lads you seem to be enjoying yourselves, how about a few carols to round off this joyous day in the Holy Land?

Well put like that how could we refuse. There were the rousing ones like Hark the Herald Angles sing, Good King Wenceslas but the one I think that really hit us was Silent Night. They sang softly and at times a little croakily, and the picture that carol conjured up, snow on the roofs of our homes back in England, carol singers at the door, Mum and Dad and the family, made it a little difficult to sing with a few watery eyes. I think we were glad the Padre came in with his carols, it was like going home for a couple of hours. Now it is back to our tents, Happy Christmas.

I think he had another reason for coming into the naafi, he wants to get up a party for a visit to Jerusalem, and he has asked all those interested to give their names to company office, I think I shall have some of that.

He has a little difficulty rounding up his flock, although his church is always full on Sundays, but this is mainly due to the fact that a squad is detailed to attend church parade each Sunday, no excuses. I tried what my Dad told me but it did not work, Dad said just tell them you are Baptist, I did and the sergeant said right you can stand outside, I found the service very interesting!

Ten of us have put our names down for the Jerusalem trip we are in the back of the truck and the Padre up front with the driver. Just as well as our conversation might be a little different fo from his.

It is a sunny day the country is looking green and pleasent with some of the orange crop still to be picked. The Padre seems to have friends in high places (no not that high) he knows the manager of the "King David Hotel" a most impressive building.

It is built with large blocks of stone very clean, looking almost newly built, we have refreshments here before going into the city.

The inner city is very old with very narrow street and Arab craftsmen making and selling their goods. Now onto the route of the crucifixion and to the church where Christ was born, very plain from the outside, but beautiful inside, we are now taken through the church to the spot where his birth took place.

There is of course absolute silence and we try to cast our minds back to that time, so many years ago and with the war and it's death and destruction having ended only two years ago, it was a little difficult to do.

We come out of the church through the very small door about five feet high and make our way to the last place of interest as we must soon head back to camp.

This is the Garden of Gethsemane, it is a rather stony area, and lay in a slight valley, and we are now standing at the side of this area looking down. There are shrubs scattered around, quite well spaced out, not thickly wooded and in amongst them a number of very old Yew Trees.

We stand here in silence looking down at this rather barren area bathed in sunlight, twelve of us in absolute silence, not a word is said, we were absorbing the intense feeling of being here where Jesus walked with his disciples all those years ago, perhaps for the last time.

We are brought back down to earth by our guide who tells us that if we would like a certificate of pilgrimage it will be one shilling. This is still one of my treasured possessions.

We are on our way back now it has been a wonderful trip, one I feel priviledged to have made. Back at camp the Padre thanks us all for making the trip with him ,have you enjoyed it?: yes sir we certainly have, so have I he says, thank you again lads good night.

I am at work today but I am making an excuse to visit company office as today names are being drawn for food parcels which are then sent directly from Australia to our homes in the U K. I walk into the office and the captain says what are you doing here Hawn? I've come to see the draw done sir, he looked a trifle annoyed, and then said well, you had better do it then. I put my hand in the box pulled out a paper and handed it to the sergeant and he read out the name. The name is Hawn!

I was ready to burst out laughing, but it was obvious I would be the only one so I just smiled. The captain said I don't know how you did it Hawn but congratulations, I hope your family enjoy it, Thank you sir, and I was off out the door before they linched me.

A nice little skive today a trip to base depot to pick up supplies for the workshops.

Things are hotting up a bit in Palestine now and all the trucks have armed escorts, and today I am it! and its
great to get out of camp. The problem is that it has been decided that part of Palestine shall become a Jewish state which will be called Israel, and we now have too see that the numbers of immigrants coming in are carefully regulated.

In the government in London it must have seemed quite simple, just say now, now old chap wait your turn, and they would walk down the gang plank like sheep, not likely, these guys had different ideas.
The ships coming here were loaded with refugees from war torn Europe and we were refusing them immediate entry, and so the inevitable terrorist groups were formed the Irgun and the

Stern. These people had come thousands of miles they could see the promised land, and they would have their part of it. They would give no thought to the plight of the Arabs of Palestine that they were displacing.

Dealing with terrorists is a rather one sided affair, we are in uniform but they are not. In this situation we only know our enemy when he fires the gun or pulls the pin on his hand granade, a bit late. To even things up a bit our rifles have been replaced with American Thompson sub machine guns, a much better gun, if you get the chance to use it, but we only get it on escort duty. Uneventful this time but it made a day out, think I'll have some more of that.

Near mutiny this morning, It's breakfast time and we have porridge, half a grapefruit, a sausage, and two slices of bread, each slice has about twenty brown weevils in it and we assume we are expected to eat it. The noise is quite deafening but now we will get some action, the duty officer has arrived.
As he passes I stand up, excuse me Sir, yes that is it? the bread Sir, it is full of weevils are we expected to eat it? At this point the orderly sergeant bawls out, quiet! and the officer speaks.

He says he is aware of the problem but there is nothing he can do about it, are we expected to eat it Sir? another man asks, that is up to you, I cannot alter the situation, but tomorrow the situation will be resolved. He turns to me and say's does that answer your question? Yes Sir. As he moves away Steve stands up, excuse me Sir, yes what is it this time? does the bread in the officers mess have weevils Sir? what a sight, this pompous product of the officer training college looking down at the lowest of ranks, an ordinary private who has dared to suggest that conditions in the officers mess are different from his own, the officer turns and walks away, Steve does not get an answer. I did not push my point too much as it was this officer who placed me on a charge for fighting in the dining hall, not really a fight more a disagreement,

The seats in the dining hall are marble slabs a trifle cold in the morning when you only have a pair of cotton shorts on your behind. Ginger came in and placed his cushion on the seat he was the only guy who had a cushion and of course was a target for amusement. He went up to get his breakfast and I sat on the cushion when he came back I expected him to say move over mate, but he proceeded to move me and I responded. The charge was disorderly conduct.

Here we are outside compny office and in we go. The C.S.M. bawls out "escort and the accused quick march" left right, left right, left right, halt, hats off. Right say's the commanding officer you are charged with disorderly conduct, do you accept my punishment, yes sir, seven days C.B. carry on sergeant major most cases were quickly processed.
Confined to barracks (C B) did not mean a lot as the camp was out in the wilds, but it was what went with it. Parade with the guard at guard mounting at 6pm, after which change into overalls and report to the cook house for cleaning duties, on parade for guard dismount at 6a.m, then off to work. My opponent and I are now quite friendly and I think we will avoid any more of that.

The commanding officer is a fitness fanatic and has ordered one hours drill each morning from 5-30 to 6-30 before breakfast, but it is not all bad as he has made available two trucks to take us swimming at Nathanya beach, I can't swim but that is the place to learn.

Two men have to stay with the trucks and guns, but one of them would never go in the water anyway. The trips to the beach were great and on the way back we would stop by a water melon field an help ourselves to a few, they were as big as footballs, dark green and scarlet inside, delicious. There were usually a few shouts from the owners but the field was full of melons, and any way what happened a couple of night ago more than paid for a few melons.

It was pay day and most of the lads kept their money in their pockets, but me being a little more suspicious put mine under my pillow, but like I have said there are a few thieving swines about and it pays to remember that. Next morning their money was gone, mine was still under my pillow.

Today I had one of the best laughs I have had for ages. It was dinner time and we were all seated round this six feet square of marble eating our dinner, on the table would usually be salt, pepper and mustard, today there is no mustard. The duty officer now approaches our table and asks, any complaints? Yes sir I said, no mustard, he moved on to the next table and I thought no more of it I really only said it to get a laugh but it turned out quite a laugh indeed.

From the serving area there are now three cooks heading my way their arms at shoulder height, each with something in their hands, this turns out to be a pot of mustard. They make their way to my table with their eyes firmly fixed on me and as they pass me each one thrashes his pot of mustard down on the marble table with a sound like that of three rifle shots. The three about turn and head back to the cook house still with their arms held out in front of them like three Egyptian sand dancers, by now the dining area was full of laughing choking men, even the duty officer had a grin. I guess the show was on me but everyone enjoyed the floor show including me.

I have been in the army a couple of years now and have never annoyed the cooks, but a couple of days later I did it again, this time I don't think it was my fault. Dinner again and it was fish, I hold my plate out and a piece of fish is placed it, and a rather small piece. I looked at the fish and up to the cook, but it had no effect, the duty officer stood by the bench and I repeated the process, :I looked down at the fish, and up at the officer, and the officer said, give that man another piece of fish. I enjoyed the fish, but my popularity in the cook house has dropped somewhat.

The green fields of Palestine are now turning brown as the temperature goes up. In October the weather breaks and the rain begins, the weather then becomes like our English summer, showers and bright periods, but by April it is warming up and summer begins with long hot days.

Now in some of the field the only green is that of those football sized water melons which are now ripe, the orange trees are still very dark green with glossy leaves and small dark green oranges, they are kept in good condition by water which is pumped up from below ground, the fruit will be picked in December.

It is quite amusing when we have a football match to see where we have sat under an orange tree, little piles of orange peel all around.

Today we are having another day out as the Padre has organised a trip to Damascus, Syria, It is not just to get out of camp, I really want to see all I can. We have set our very early and we are about to take the winding road that rises above Gallilea, and the sea of Gallilee sparkles like diamonds in the early morning light. On the water are fishing vessels presenting a beautiful peaceful sight, I guess they were up long before us.

Up and up along this winding road, almost mesmerized by the scene below and not a terrorist in sight. At the top now and the sea below looks quite distant, but here at the Syrian border there are wild tulips, and in the distance are snow capped mountains. It's begining to look like a great trip.

The road to Damascus was not so spectacular, but the city quite impressed me, it seemed so modern for a mid East city, and the Padre was able to point out items of historical and biblical interest. Our journey home presented no problems though I did find the road down into Palestine a little scary as it was almost dark and the road seemed a little narrower, and nearer the edge. Back at camp the Padre thanks us for coming on the trip, but I think it is we who should thank him, it was interesting and enjoyable.

After that trip and the news I have had today I am almost glad I joined. A number of us have been told that we qualify for LIAP, which represents a months leave in England. It seems incredible that after only eighteen months out here I will be taken back to England for a months leave but I am not complaining It is August and mighty hot and we are going aboard our ship, she looks great, what a ship, quite big, twenty two thousand tons, I think I am going to enjoy this.

It's like a civilian cruise liner, there is a hugh lounge with settees, and arm chairs, books on the tables. and fans above, but still with those perishing hammocks. We spend our days up on deck playing cards and now and again the Captain will speak over the loud speaker system as we pass another ship. "We are not passing the S S---- outward bound from Liverpool, bound for ----". It was just like a civilian cruise.

Today we might all wish we were some place else, there are waves as high as the bridge, and even this big ship is being tossed around, we find it hard to believe, a storm as bad as this in the Med. Every where there are men being sick, the stench was awful, and men green with sea sickness were definitly a reality. No cards on deck today, just brooms and scrubbing brushes.

Back to normal today the "card school" is back in business, what a way to be a soldier, up on deck soaking up the sun, playing cards.

A little disappointing today as we pass Gibralter, it is shrouded in mist, but we were very relieved with the Bay of Biscay it was like a mill pond. The best sight of today, England, unfortunatly our port of disembarkation is Glasgow, so I have to go all the way up the West Coast by ship and then all the way back down to Kent by train.

We enter the Clyde, green grass on both sides, not a desert in sight, fantastic, and I think of the words of the poet.

Be there a man with soul so dead
Who never to himself has said
This is mine own, my native land.

It may be Scotland, but to me it is Britain, the land of the Union Jack.

We get a great welcome from the Scots, and they tell us what they would like to do with those Jewish terrorists. They have heard about the murder of two army sergeants in Palestine.

The terrorists took these two sergeants of the education corp hostage and tried to swap them for two terrorists that we held, obviously we could not do this, and so the two sergeants were hung in a eucalyptus grove, Murdered.

It was all the more dispicable when we thought of the British army racing across Germany to release Jews that were about to die in the gas chambers, now it is shoot to kill!

Well farewell Scotland I'm heading south to the garden of England, Kent where Ashford lies. I guess the train is going quite fast the wheels are going clikety clack clikety clack but it seems a hell of a way from Glasgow to Kent. After several sleeps we are in London, across now to Waterloo and on to the train for Ashford, and here we are I recognize that voice, Ashford, slow and leisurly, my old market town.

A great reception at home from Mum and Dad, only they are at home at the moment, Ern is married and gone, Bill is also married Les is home from Italy, and now at work, Herby also at work harvesting, Reg is in the RAF, conscription is still in force, and Derek and Rita are at work.

It was great to be home, and we had a good chat, but the family have things to do and my mates are away in the army and so it soon became less exciting, Food rationing is still in force and still a little un interesting, but there was always walks to the Warren with Tinker our dog. The September weather is marvellous and I am off on such a trip.
Not much has changed the County School girls are still doing their P.T and I pause to admire their actions, but Tinker shows no interest, on a bit further and the grass has almost covered the position of the anti-aircraft gun, up the hill and into the Warren. The ferns are almost brown now but it still has that magical silence where one can make plans for the next fifty years, and the only sand I see is in the bunkers on the golf links. Egypt is far away.

This weekend my mates Charlie and Bill have a weekend pass and we are at the Corn Exchange dance, not so much for the dancing, but a few drinks, and lots of laughs, but of course lots of laughs were accompanied by lots of drinks and when we left the dance hall our main concern was, which one was most in need of assistance home.
After much slurred debating it was decided it should be done in alphabetical order, and as H came before R I was delivered and I hoped all the neighbours were asleep, for as they went off singing.

We shall tell the Sergeant Major to poke his passes up his, the slurred words made the last work difficult to catch.

They have gone back to camp now and they will not get another pass for a few weeks, and I am beginning to look forward to going back myself. It has been nice to be home but I have to admit to "ever so slight" boredom, and I am glad tomorrow I go back.

I big hug for Mum, a firm shake of the hand from Dad, a wave for the gang and I am off, as I turn the corner I turn and wave and I am on my way back to Palestine.

I know it seems strange, a months holiday, no guards, pickets, or other duties, but boredom made me restless and I am glad to be back in harness. I still marvel at being brought three thousand miles home and now I am going the same distance back. I am not complaining.

We had assembled on the race course at Liverpool, and will soon be boarding our ship, this one is nothing like the one we came home on. I don't think it will make it! We have cast off heading out to sea all the way down the West coast, past the Scilly Isles, the Bay of Biscay is calm again, Portugal with its red soil and Gibralter looked great, and we are now in the Med, but we are now in Algiers for repairs. We don't know what kind of repairs but with our deck being below the water line, I hope it's not the hull.

Off again and the old ship is making it's way through the Blue water in lovely warm sunshine while we play cards on deck.
I am now in no hurry to get back, more trouble with the old boat, and we put in to Malta, still it all delays our arrival back at camp, a couple of days yet before we dock at Port Said.
We are back now and we are soon off the boat and onto the train bound for Haifa Palestine.

We are met by our truck and learn that our base is now on Mount Carmel, and off we go up the narrow road with a long drop if we go over the edge, at this time I can't drive just hope that the guy behind the wheel can. At the top it looks quite promising, sort of permanent, and when we went to the cookhouse we got the impression that the commanding officer had a good sense of humour. There over the door in big red letters were the words, The Airborne is a shower, The Airborne is a farce, take your cherry beret and stuff it up your ----, not a Sandhurst trained officer obviously!

The words obviously referred to the Airborne Division that had been here before, and I had to admire the commanding officer for leaving it up there, my kind of guy!

The Airborne Divisions were first rate soldiers, they had to be, they were the spearhead of most major battles, but because of this they had a very good opinion of themselves. and were not too well liked by other units.

My lot, REME workshops, electricians, carpenters, coach painters etc, bore very little resemblence to the Airborne soldier, and this inflated ego, but we also had a job to do, transport was essential, and trucks on the road make fine targets for aircraft, unless the driver had some one in the back he would never know until the bullets came tearing into his truck.

It is Sunday afternoon and we are on our bunks, some writing home, some reading, some just snoozing, but one guy thinks he will liven things up a bit.

A Hornet has just come in, they are about one and a half inches long and as thick as a pencil, and Don is watching it as it flies around, it has now found one of our water bottles and in it goes. Don hops off his bunk grabs the metal water bottle and shoves the stopper in, by now we all have a rough idea of what comes next and quickly get our mosquito nets in position. Don slowly unrolls his mosquito net reaches for the bottle gives it a jolly good shake and with it outside his net removes the stopper, it flies around looking for someone to vent it's anger on and then goes out the door, and all is quiet again. This has rather broken my concentration and so when Len comes in and asks me if I want a game of cards, well that was the end of letter writing.

Our favourite place for a card game is the telephone hut, on a Saturday night as it is a bit out of the way and does not get a visit from the duty officer, The guy on telephone duty sleeps in the hut by the phone, or should I say tries to. Not much chance really as the card game is usually Pontoon and so all evening he will hear calls like, money on your cards, what are you doing Fred? I'm sticking, I'll twist says Ray, Jim say's buy one, and another, and again, stick five carder, right say's the banker turning his cards over, pay nineteens, and off we go again.

It is eleven o'clock and I am broke "Maffish Falouse" I say (Arabic for no money) I'm out, no don't pack in, here is a tanner says Jim, and with that sixpence I went on to finish up with Two pounds fifty. As it was gone I-30 we decided to pack it in and get to our bunks. I go carefully through the door, not a sound and then when I get to my bunk I kick my neighbours steel kit box with my canvas shoes, "Cor sod that" I let out as I lurched forward crashing into the bunk above mine, this woke Angus, and looking at me he bawles out "well go on man make some ruddy noise why don't you". By now the whole hut is awake, it is nearly half past ruddy one say's another guy, I know, I know, sorry lads and with much mumbling it quietens down with just snores and grunts and all is well, but I expect to hear more in the morning. Well they let me off light in the morning and as I am on guard tonight they will have a quieter night.

Since being here on Mount Carmel I have found one good thing about guards, I can get a cold drink. Up here the surface is solid rock, and the water pipes have been laid over the rock with the result that the water become hot with the heat of the sun and a drink of hot water is awful, at night on guard in the early hours of the morning I can go into the wash house and have a marvellous drink of cold water.

This guard has been quite exciting, Captain Rintod has come into the guard room in his usual state (sozzeld) and sat on the table, he takes out his revolver and does a bit of John Wayne stuff, but it has gone off and wounded the guard commander, in the arm, I reckon Captain Rintod will soon be on his way back to the U K.

The terrorists are still busy, we have had our tents shot up, railways blown up, wire stretched across the road to catch our dispatch riders, and worst of all those two unarmed sergeants who were murdered by hanging them in a Eucalyptus grove. I think however todays cowardly act was probably the most despicable.

We had gone down into Haifa for the afternoon, and our first stop was the Naafi club on Kingsway for a cup of tea and a cake. This was up on the second floor, a nice area with a good atmosphere, relaxing. After about half an hour there was a loud explosion and the windows came in ,we tore off downstairs, but I remembered the kilo of sultanas I had left upstairs and so I quickly went back to get them.

Across the road was the terrorists target. The Palestine Police H Q, they had driven the truck load of explosive into the yard and detonated it, and now the police and service men are pulling out the dead and injured, It is even more despicable when one remembers that a couple of years ago some of these soldiers were carrying Jews from inside camps in Germany where they would have been put to death by gas chamber, gratitude has a short memory.

The terrorists could not know that in years to come their children and their children's children would also receive their bombs, also delivered by truck or bus, this time by the Arabs that had become refugees when Israel was formed, It will be an eye for an eye, a tooth for a tooth, but as Ghandi said, t his process simply means that both participants become blind, it achieves nothing!

The Palestinian police bombing was a couple of weeks ago and we are again down here in Haifa, it is always good to get out of camp. Haifa is a nice place, largely built of stone blocks of a sandy colour and in the sunlight it looks so clean and the people are O K, it is just the terrorists who spoil the picture.
Today my mate and I have walked round the back streets to see the other half, no fear of terrorists in daylight, they would not pick a fight face to face.

On our way we come upon a group of Arabs, they are sitting staring at us and we had our eyes fixed on them, we had our sten guns and could have quickly wiped them out, but we would have opened on ants nest and would not have escaped. Instead we called out "Syeeda Offeendi" and this was quickly returned "Syeeda Offendi" with a smile, and all was well.

We had no quarrel with the Arabs, I think they knew we were doing our best to hold back hordes of Jewish immigrants from their land, Palestine, and that we were being shot at for our trouble, we were doing what Whitehall U K said we must do.

The navy had a better deal, from our camp up on Mount Carmel we can see the destroyers patroling the coast line, up and down the coast looking for immigrant ships. It is hot up here but they are on the lovely blue water, with a sea breeze and just Brits for company, and should they meet an immigrant ship a boarding party will explain to the Captain his responsibilities, and return to the destroyer, job done.

The navy does it's best, but at night they are still coming ashore, and next day we try and round them up, still not for much longer.

My demob number has come up and I should be going home but not much chance of that, there are a lot of guys well overdue.

The feeling in the camp is running a little high. Quite often now when a man is threatened with punishment he will reply "I'm allakeefic" (I could'nt care less) and no action will be taken, the camp feeling is well known to the officers.

When our demob number comes up we should go home, but Whitehall U.K does not send our replacements, though they were quick enough to threaten us with imprisonment if we did not report for duty, and go to the army camp for training back home.

This feeling has existed for a year or so now and my previous camp coupled with an overbearing Commanding Officer, it boiled over. A straw that broke the Camel's back, and the guys had had enough, this fitness fanatic and die hard disciplinarian Major Gorton had pushed them too far.

Thirty men climbed into a large truck and headed for the Egyptian border, such was the feeling that it did not matter what happened now. They were of course stoped at the border and brought back under escort, they were told that they would be charged with mutiny, and all of course shouted loud and clear, I could'nt care less.

The Major now realised that if he proceeded the whole camp might mutiny, and so no charges were brought, after that things improved, but while our numbers came up, we did not go home.

Rumour has it now that demob numbers will not matter as we shall all be going home. The state of Isreal is about to be born but I won't hold my breath.

In preparation for going home, I am getting at bit of driving pratice in, I get the driver to let me have a go, but today when he said "have a go Huck" I declined. We had just started the climb up the winding road round Mount Carmel and looking over the side it was going to be a long drop, have a go, you can do it he said, no thanks mate I said, I am too near demob, and so are you.

The guy was one of the old soldiers who had fought many battles and was just a little "bomb happy", great guys but their experiances had given them an unhealthy view of risk, and dangerous situations, and with me at the wheel, we would have both been in one.

I liked these old sweats they were not yes sir, no sir guys, if they were given a stupid order they said what they thought and often it was changed. In battle they would have instantly carried out the order no hesitation, but the last battle was almost three years ago and the situation has changed. We now have young conscript N C Os passing on orders from lily white officers straight from officer training college. I can take it, but these guys who have more years service find it a little hard.

I was pleased last night that the company sergeant major inspecting the guard was also an old soldier and probably felt like the rest of us. As he came by me he said "you have not shaved" I said I have, you have not shaved he said, I repeated "I have" this was again repeated and by now I knew that the next move was his, he would have me charged with insubordination and slung in the guard room. I think perhaps because he was an old soldier and also wanted to go home that he let us both off the hook by saying, well, stand closer to the razor next time, yes sir! phew that was close.

Well it is all coming too an end now, we came here to regulate Jewish immigration but it has become almost impossible, we cannot keep them out and so we are pulling out, our job is done.

We are getting our camps in order, and that will allow us to leave this beautiful but very uneasy country, as soon as Whitehall says so.

That directive has now been received, we leave in one week and we are all very pleased about that, well most of us, some of course must stay until the state of Israel is offically born on May 16th 1948.

The terrorists cannot wait too see the back of us, but I think most of the Jewish population see it a little differently,

The Jewish shop keepers in Kingsway Haifa, especially, as one of them told me it would hit his jewellery business badly.

Well here we are at the docks with our ship waiting to take us home, which is great, but I feel this old trooper will not make it by the thirteenth, when I shall be twenty one.
Twenty one at that time was the age when it was thought a boy became a man. I've had to laugh at times when I thought of the times when I could have been killed, and still not termed a man.

We are on board ship now and lining the rails down below on the docks we are being given the full treatment. The Millitary band in full ceremonial uniform are playing us off, not in parade ground stuff, but more sentimental pieces like "Will ye nay come back again" and although we all want to get home it is a little quiet on deck.

It is really a bit of a tear jerker as we pull away from the dock, the guys down there give us a cheer and we return it. They must stay for the hand over when Israel is born, and Palestine becomes a little smaller, and another refugee situation is brought about. It has been a little scarey at times in Palestine, but it is a beautiful country especially about April, May and I am glad to have had the opportunity to be here.

It has been great to sit under the orange trees eating the fruit, bathed in the warm Mediterranean, stood guard in the middle of the night and watched an electric storm, all very memorable.

Palestine is becoming a little more distant and the ceremonial gathering has dispersed. We have tried to do the job we were sent here to do, to bring about a peaceful transition, but we found it hard to understand why Arabs must leave to make way for the Jews. It seemed totally against our democratic way of life Still ours is not to reason why, ours is but to do or die, be good soldiers, and do as we were ordered.

As Palestine fades into the distance it become obvious that our presence here did very little good in stopping the flood of immigrants, and was not that successful, but I guess it satisfied the concience of those who dreamed up the idea, but I wonder how that fits in with the displaced Arabs,

It is all over for us now and we have our card school going, roll on England and we promise never to join anything ever again, not even a christmas club.
Being early March the weather is not too good but guess the nearer we get to the U K it gets colder and wetter, but at the moment the U K weather will do fine.

The ship is full of Army, Navy and Air Force personal, we are down below, officers and wives have the upper decks, the class system is not yet dead, at the stern end are the guys who man the ship, they are a good bunch always good for a laugh.

The thought of getting out of the Army is great, but then another thought say's "what then"? do I want to go back to spraying paint, well I have a month or two in which to decide, but at the moment the sea is calm and the days are easy, right now we are passing through the Straits of Gibralter and I think to myself "I may never pass this way again."

There are some things I shall not forget about the sea trips like three hundred men below decks for the night, it was always good to get up on deck for some fresh air. Another would be the memory of that smell when three hundred men in the dining area also below decks opened their boiled eggs, I never was keen on eggs, and that did it.

Through the Bay of Biscay again, this is the third time and it's calm again, I thought it was supposed to be rough!

It is the thirteenth, and I am twenty one today, I would like to have got home for it, but if Bill and Charlie can get a weekend pass we will still celebrate.

Land Ahoy and it's England, unfortunatly we dock at Liverpool, and that is a fair way up the coast, and it's raining. Liverpool and down the gang plank we go, the trucks are waiting and we are off t our last army camp, but this is the one we have all been waiting to get to.

Here we will be medically examined and kitted out for civilian life, We have a good nights sleep on bunks, not hammocks, and we are ready to be transformed from soldiers to civilians, We go into this massive building which is like a giant Burton's the tailors, there is a very good selection from socks, to raincoats and no pressure to make up our minds, as soldiers we always had our minds made up for us.

I have chosen a blue serge suit, black shoes, and a stone coloured raincoat, plus socks, and under cloths, tie and a trilby hat. I look like a book makers runner, this is now in a nice cardboard box ready for the new me.

It is now back to our bunks to change, and then to hand our uniforms boots etc, into the quarter master, not forgetting our "housewife" which is a canvas wallet with darning needles and wool for repairs to our socks.

What a sight! hundreds of men, all in spanking new cloths of many different colours moving round the army camp, the camp was on Aintree race course and that was what it looked like. Into the cook house for dinner, after which we must be on the square for the final push out of the gates.

It is strange to be sitting here here in the cook house still in the army but all around are people in civilian cloths, we have to smile, we look so different from the boys they took from Mum three years ago. We look a little older, a little wiser. and a great deal more cynical, but I think they have done what they said they would do, turned us into men.

It is a strange feeling, I thought it would be marvellous, the feeling of escape, but it is not, it is the realization that once through that gate I am on my own to think for myself, sink or swim, and I will swim!.

We are on the square now all lined up and when my name is called I shall march smartly to my position, that's my name and here I go.

At the table sits an officer and I march smartly up to him but I do not salute him, as I am now not in uniform, he looks up does a faint smile and say's his piece.

Well Hawn I expect you are happy to be getting back to your job, and home life, but I hope you do not consider your time in the army wasted, we most definitly do not. Your time in Palestine was certainly not wasted, and to mark its importance each participant of that period of service will receive a medal which you will receive in due course.

Well Hawn here are your documents, railway warrent, ration book which you will require in civilian life, and I wish you all the best in that life. He puts his hand forward to shake hands, I turn smartly to my right, and head for the trucks that will take us to the rail station, but still I cannot feel that sense of freedom, escape, release! I think I have become a soldier and an going into a strange new world.

Not to worry I am going home, and if I spray paint or fly an aircraft, it will be down to me not some guy with stripes on his arm, or pips on his shoulder who quite often was unworthy of them.

Through the gate and now I am Mr Hawn, I think I shall dispose of Huckleberry and use my second name Frank.

Mr Frank Hawn, I like that, I have always been just a little frank my nature.

Our first 21 years have come and gone, the tragedy of those years must not return. For while we look forward to our "next stories" we remember those whose stories will never be told.

The excitement now will be of girl friends, wives, children, mortgages, over drafts, university tuition fees – ETC.

I wonder if they will take me back?

Printed in the United Kingdom by
Lightning Source UK Ltd., Milton Keynes
137434UK00002B/130-177/P